ALDABRA

or

Translated by LYNNE SHARON SCHWARTZ

the

Tortoise

Who

Loved

Shakespeare

by Silvana Gandolfi

Arthur A. Levine Books

AN IMPRINT OF SCHOLASTIC INC.

Library of Congress Cataloging-in-Publication Data
Gandolfi, Silvana.
[Aldabra, la tartaruga che amava Shakespeare. English]
Aldabra, or, The tortoise who loved Shakespeare / by Silvana Gandolfi ; translated by Lynne Sharon Schwartz. — 1st American ed.
    p. cm.
Summary: In Venice, Italy, ten-year-old Elisa finds she must deal with all the unexpected consequences of her beloved eccentric grandmother's transformation into a giant Aldabra tortoise, native to a small group of coral islands in the Seychelles.
ISBN 0-439-49741-8
[1. Grandmothers — Fiction. 2. Mothers and daughters — Fiction. 3. Aldabra tortoise — Fiction. 4. Turtles — Fiction. 5. Human-animal relationships — Fiction. 6. Magic — Fiction. 7. Venice (Italy) — Fiction. 8. Italy — Fiction.] I. Title: Tortoise who loved Shakespeare. II. Schwartz, Lynne Sharon. III. Title.
PZ7.G1466A1 2004
[Fic] — dc22

                                                          2003016858

10 9 8 7 6 5 4 3 2 1   04 05 06 07 08
Printed in the U.S.A.   37
First American edition, April 2004

To Donatella,
companion of all my travels
in the realms of the impossible

—S. G.

Chapter One

"The way to outsmart death, Elisa dear, is to transform yourself."

Every time she murmured those words, Nonna Eia would open her brown eyes wide and gaze at me intently. Her faint foreign accent grew more pronounced and her voice seemed to hover over some mysterious abyss. I stayed taut as the string of a bow, holding my breath, my lips parted, and stared right back at her. It was a contest to see whose eyes could open wider.

After a moment of suspense, my grandmother would grasp my hands and, in a whisper scented with jasmine and spices, start telling me her favorite legend. That was six years ago, but still, to this day, if I recall the delicate, aromatic fragrance that floated on her breath as she spoke, all the events of that time spring forth intact. The scent of jasmine is like a long thread that draws back to me not a kite or something flying high in the sky, but the great adventure of my childhood.

Nonna Eia's legend was about an ancient people at the far ends of the earth where the women could choose never to die.

They had the power to change into something new. That was the way to cheat death: The trick was to be transformed. It was no easy trick, though, and not everyone could manage it. She'd tried it herself once, but it hadn't worked out very well. In fact, she had to confess she'd "screwed up," she had said with a chuckle.

"What did you want to change into, Nonna?"

"I can't remember."

"A mermaid?" I suggested, thinking of the pictures Nonna painted. One of her favorite subjects was those girls with silvery fish tails dancing on the sky-blue waves.

"A mermaid? Now that you mention it, yes, I think you're right. No wonder I couldn't do it. I'm not even sure mermaids really exist!" She chuckled again, then turned serious. "The thing is, Elisa, you can only transform yourself into something that's already part of your innermost nature."

Nonna Eia could tell stories or legends as if they were precious secrets, matters of life or death. She had the special gift of making you believe in her stories; the wilder they were, the more tantalizingly real they felt.

My grandmother always dressed in white, summer and winter. She had come to Venice from England at twenty years old and instantly "fell like a ripe apple" into the arms of a worker at the shipyard — he became my mother's father. She married him without a moment's hesitation, even though she had to give up her promising career as an actress in London. Then her husband died, leaving her alone with a small baby. To get by, Eia began painting pretty scenes of Venice, the kind you see on boxes of chocolates, to sell to tourists. She never left the city again.

I went to see her almost every day. From my house to hers took about half an hour. Walking fast.

Up until the Celestia pier, there was never any problem.

But beyond the pier, when I reached the metal footbridge alongside the high brick wall, I started walking faster.

The old shipyard wall was covered with crude murals in lurid colors that reminded me of war, so whenever I walked along the narrow bridge I kept my head turned toward the lagoon so as not to see them. Below the bridge, at low tide, there'd be a narrow stretch of mud and debris — crumbling bricks coated with seaweed, rusty garbage cans, gutted car seats. It seemed like the tide might bring in anything, not just garbage. I would scan that pathetic excuse for a beach for anything special or shiny. I'd stare especially hard at the bottles, trying to see behind the dirty glass to what was inside. Could they contain a message? If only I could greet Nonna Eia with a letter from a shipwrecked castaway from the other end of the world. She'd really appreciate something like that.

Of course I'd never gone down there to check the bottles more closely. The planks of rotten wood, a little farther on, were enough to turn me off. They were lopsided as drunkards, sticking out in the murky water just across from the island with the cemetery. They gave me weird ideas. Like, what if the head of some drowned person was hidden beneath that putrid seaweed under the piers?

Halfway across the footbridge, my legs started running of their own accord. When I passed the big shed with the boarded-up windows, I never even peeked through the cracks in the bricks. Once in a while, though, I took advantage of a moment when people were passing by to have a quick look inside. If I wasn't all alone, I had enough nerve to stop. I would press my face up against the wire netting that covered the cracks and try to devour everything inside with my eyes as fast as I could. The roof was extremely high, with cracks that let in enough light so I could make out the ground, overgrown with shrubs and weeds. Mysterious stone fireplaces were lined up against the walls. Fireplaces gigantic enough to roast a whole ox. A trace of sunlight filtered through some of them, a pale imitation of the fires that once blazed there.

This shed was much bigger than the one Nonna Eia used as a studio. Bigger and emptier. Creepier. The perfect setting for nighttime meetings of the Ku Klux Klan.

There was no one passing by that day, so I didn't slow down until the end of the footbridge, when I caught sight of the *Casermette*. A few of these narrow row houses were lived in,

{ 4 }

with small, well-kept gardens full of roses. But in most of them, the windows had been barred for years and there were brambles outside, not roses. Along the seawall of the lagoon there was always laundry hanging on a long line: underwear, socks, stiff old pants that snapped in the wind. The same laundry, week after week, it seemed to me.

Once in a great while I'd see people outside, puttering around the houses. Sometimes they might give me a quick nod. They were all old people. There were very few children, and those few were very bashful. If I slowed down to watch them play, they'd hurry up and move away, not smiling and not hostile. So I'd learned never to stop.

The *Casermette* were a brief oasis of relative calm. The scariest part of the trip was still to come.

That day, as so often before, I felt like Little Red Riding Hood going through the dangerous woods to visit her grandmother. And just like Little Red Riding Hood, I was bringing her food that was cooked with love. It wasn't tucked in a straw basket but in a plastic bag. So far I'd never come across any wolf.

And yet isn't it strange, I thought that day. Mamma never comes with me. Doesn't she ever think it might be dangerous? Hasn't she seen how wild and isolated it is out here? No, that was the point. She'd never seen it.

All of a sudden two thoughts were colliding in my head.

The first was: I have the perfect grandmother. Poor and

totally lovable. Smells of jasmine flowers. Great at telling stories. She believes everything I say and never scolds. Who wouldn't want a grandmother like that?

The second thought was: Mamma, who's Nonna Eia's only daughter, never crosses the metal footbridge to visit her. And Nonna Eia, who has no other family in the world, never comes to see us. Never never never. Not even at Christmas. They never even talk on the phone.

This last fact was understandable: Nonna didn't have a phone. But it didn't explain the rest.

How peculiar that I'd never thought about it. I was so used to going by myself, Red Riding Hood all alone, traipsing off to see her grandmother. I'd been going since I was big enough; before that, neighbors used to take me, friends of Mamma's. I'd never noticed what an odd arrangement this was.

How many times had I gone to see Nonna Eia? Figure four afternoons a week, then you'd have to multiply four by fifty-two, which made about two hundred times a year. Then two hundred times ten, because that's how old I was then, and I'd been going for my entire life. That made two thousand times. But you'd have to subtract the months right after I was born, when I was too small to be taken on such a long walk, and then the time when I had scarlet fever, and school trips and other holidays. . . . It was safe to say that I had gone to see Nonna at least fifteen hundred times.

And every time without my mom!

And I'd never found it strange.

Maybe habits don't seem strange as long as they're habits —
especially if you've had them from the time you were born.

That day, though, I couldn't stop thinking of how it just
didn't make sense. Maybe it was because before I got to Celestia I ran into Francesca, my friend from school, walking between her mother and her grandmother. Her grandmother was
really really old — ninety-four. And still, the three of them
were going along happily together, on their way to the depart-
ment store to get Francesca a new dress.

I went on, lost in thought, leaving behind the small gardens and the laundry flapping in the wind, crossing overgrown
lots thick with tall grass, nettles, and every kind of tangled
undergrowth.

What secret rule could be keeping Nonna and Mamma,
mother and daughter, from seeing each other? What was it that
I didn't know? Whenever I got back home, Mamma would in-
terrogate me about Nonna Eia's health. She bombarded me
with questions, sometimes embarrassing ones. Like, "Did she
have a strange smell? Are you sure she's keeping clean?"

She was concerned about Nonna Eia. She loved her. So
why were they avoiding each other?

I reached the massive arch in the wall with the huge letters
rising above it: VENICE SHIPYARD.

Once I was past the archway, the lagoon was out of sight, hidden by the high wall, crenellated like the wall of a castle, that bordered the whole area. I passed by more large red brick sheds with strange metal contraptions painted bright blue. They must have something to do with preventing corrosion. But I'd never seen anyone enter.

As I reached the sign that read MILITARY ZONE, I stared for a moment at the red cross with the little hand and a slash going across: the symbol for "do not enter." I had to turn right.

Other buildings had signs warning not to come too close: DANGER OF COLLAPSE.

I kept on going. By this time I wasn't feeling scared anymore, like Red Riding Hood in the woods. I was too busy trying to fit together everything I hadn't noticed till then. There were suddenly so many facts I couldn't explain.

For instance, Nonna Eia never mentioned her daughter's name. There were no photos of Mamma in her house. Not a single one.

Plus, whenever I told her something that involved Mamma, she would listen and not say a word. She just kept silent, with a fixed smile pasted on her face, until I stopped talking. Then she would change the subject.

Very, very, very strange. How come I never noticed before?

And another thing: Why did Mamma remind me, each time, to tell Nonna that I was the one who'd cooked the food

I was bringing? All by myself, with my own two hands. Lots of times Mamma had made it, in a big hurry, and all I contributed was the finishing touches, which sometimes turned out bizarre and complicated. But still, Mamma always warned me to say I had mixed it, I had dredged it in flour, I had put it in the oven, all by myself.

Was it to impress Nonna with my talents? That was what I'd thought so far. But now it was becoming one more peculiar fact.

I crossed the cabbage patches and reached the gate of the shipyard.

As usual, I turned left at the gate to slip into the brambles and the tall grass at just the right place. The start of the path was hidden by shrubbery; to find it you had to know exactly where to step. No one would dream of going straight into the middle of the nettles like a four-year-old kid. I checked the wild cherry saplings that grew along the path. The fruit was almost ripe. Another couple of weeks, maybe. I knew their taste very well: sour enough to make your teeth shiver. When they went from pale pink to a beautiful, translucent red, I would pick them from the branches and pop them in my mouth two or three at a time, then shoot out the pits like a volley of bullets.

After about sixty feet, the overgrown little path suddenly opened out to a broad clearing surrounded by trees. Now that it was almost summer, the clearing had a lovely carpet of grass. In the center was a mound rising six or eight feet high, like a miniature mountain. The grass was always bright green up there, even in winter — who knows why. Near the far end of the clearing were the garden and a toolshed.

I looked around. Nonna Eia might be somewhere outside, hoeing in the rows of cabbages, wearing her long white dress that magically never got dirty. I didn't see her that day, though, so I went on.

She must be inside, in the kitchen, listening to her battery-powered radio, cutting heaps of greens into tiny bits for one of her special salads. Or in the abandoned shed near the house, a shed that was identical to the one I passed after the bridge, except it was smaller and had no fireplaces inside. It was Nonna's studio and was crammed with a vast array of brushes, tubes, and jars of paint lined up on upside-down fruit crates. Even the canvases were stored on stacks of crates, to keep them safe in case of flooding. Buckets of water were positioned every which way on the floor.

I crossed the clearing, passing beneath the leafy branches of the trees, and stopped at the carcass of a broken-down boat abandoned on the grass. It must have been there for at least a century. When I was younger, I liked to hide inside the frame, playing pirates. Now I just stared at it, letting my eyes close little by little until the boat started dissolving in the mist between my half-open eyelids. And then, by concentrating hard, I could make it gradually rise up from the grass to go drifting across the sky like the basket of a hot air balloon.

Right opposite the hull of the boat was Nonna Eia's front door, made of wooden planks, once upon a time turquoise-blue. It was framed by great clusters of sprawling, clinging vines, as tangled as a jungle, that grew so densely over the drainpipes and along the walls of the house that they hid the upstairs windows, whose broken panes were held together by strips of masking tape.

The door had no doorbell. How could it? Nonna's house had no electricity.

As I did each time, before I knocked I stuck my nose in the air and gazed at the patch of sky enclosed by the high crenellated wall.

All I could see was the slender tip of a far-off church spire. Only the very tip. And a little to one side, a slight distance away, the top of a huge crane. Nothing more of Venice was visible. As far as I was concerned, the city had disappeared.

Chapter Two

The door opened and I slipped into the tiny entrance hall crammed with tall rubber boots and rain ponchos.

Nonna spread out her arms and bent down to offer her soft cheek, which smelled of jasmine and spices, like her breath. Her long white hair was gathered in a schoolgirl's braid that hung down her back. It looked like white wool.

After our kiss she held me at arm's length to have a better look. Her face took on a puzzled expression.

"Elisa, how did you get that potbelly?"

I looked down at my jeans. As a matter of fact the bulge was quite prominent. I tried to look remorseful. "Does it show already? Well, I guess I can tell *you* about it. . . . I'm in big trouble, Nonna. . . . I'm pregnant!"

For a fraction of a second my grandmother's eyes widened. I could have made her believe anything. Even so, I didn't want her falling to the floor in a faint. So I slipped my hand under my belt and started unrolling the thin white fabric, all crumpled up.

"It's my nightgown, Nonna. I wore it underneath so I could play Ophelia without wasting any time changing." I let the fabric hang down over my jeans. It was a long nightgown that reached almost to my feet.

"What a relief! So you're not expecting a baby at ten years old!" She gave an exaggerated laugh. Then she remarked, "Now we're dressed alike!"

It was true — her white dress looked like a nightgown too.

"But we need rosemary. And pansies," I said, a bit disappointed at her pretend laugh. I hadn't scared her one bit.

Nonna turned to go into the kitchen. She went over to a blue vase and took out a bunch of wildflowers and aromatic herbs. "How about these?"

"Mmm. Perfect."

I followed her into the big kitchen. Dozens of knickknacks sparkled on the shelves, along with candles, cans of coffee, and jars of flour. The burners on the stove, which was fueled by a gas tank, were gleaming. The wooden table was covered by a blue tablecloth that hid the ancient ring marks left by glasses. On the walls hung ten-year-old calendars and a few small paintings: elves, exotic almond-shaped eyes, and angels with enormous wings, all done by Nonna Eia. A slightly yellowed lace curtain hung at the window, to keep the house cozy and private.

From the small radio on a shelf came opera music, playing very softly.

I was sure my grandmother's kitchen was exactly like the ones in English cottages. Chock-full of enchanting little things — and I could touch them all, without making anyone nervous.

I set the plastic bag on the table. "For you."

"What is it?"

"Anchovy quiche."

"With the little fish heads peeking out of the crust the way I like them?"

"Yes."

"Did you make it yourself?"

It wasn't really a question, seeing that on every visit, without exception, I was quick to answer, "Sure, Nonna Eia. I made it with my very own hands. No one helped me."

That day I truly *had* made the anchovy quiche. Mamma would never have thought of stuffing it with capers, raisins, and dried fruit. And there were more pine nuts than anchovies inside. I'd stuck the fish heads on top, with their tiny open mouths. The way they popped out of the crust, it looked like they were surfacing from a pond.

"Actually I didn't have time today." I gave in to a sudden impulse to lie.

"Who made it, then?"

"Mamma."

Nonna had already reached for the bag, but she jerked back her hand as if it had been burned. For a moment she seemed to have turned to wood: a great big wooden doll dressed in white.

"I had too much homework," I explained, though my voice sounded phony even to my ears.

"I can't eat it. You have it."

"But Mamma's a fantastic cook! Much better than me!"

She turned her back and put the water on to boil. But not before I got a glimpse of her lips tightening. An ugly grimace. My sugar-and-spice grandmother with such a nasty look.

I felt guilty. But I couldn't ask, Nonna, do you and Mamma hate each other? How could I say such a thing?

I didn't know what to do next. Nonna kept quiet, her shoulders stiff and hostile. I felt like turning and running. I started babbling about the seaweed that was overrunning the lagoon again this year. What a pain! Was there that much seaweed when she was young? And so on and so forth, blah, blah, blah. I couldn't stop myself. "Have you been painting, Nonna? Did you finish the painting with the angel surrounded by flames?" Anything at all, just to take her mind off the anchovy quiche contaminated by my mother's hands.

Nonna Eia put two spoonfuls of tea in the teapot, carefully poured out the boiling water, and then, still not looking at me, turned around and placed two cups on the blue tablecloth. In silence, she set down the teapot and a plate with some cookies, pushed up a chair for me, went to turn off the radio, and finally leaned both hands on the table, as if to prop herself up. She was staring fixedly at the plastic bag. I didn't wait for her to sit down because she never did — Nonna Eia spent practically her whole life on her feet. But I was about to suggest it because she seemed so worn out.

"You should have your mamma tell you why I don't accept gifts from her. Why she and I don't see each other. I don't want to set you against your mother." She kept avoiding my eyes. "It's up to her to speak to you first. You're a big girl now, Elisa. You can think for yourself." At last, her lips curved in a small smile as she turned toward me. "Anyone who can recite Shakespeare by heart can understand all about life."

I was dumbstruck and nodded feebly. I wasn't so sure anymore if I wanted to know their secret.

Her smile broadened. "Drink your tea. Guess what? Valentina stopped by again."

Valentina was a red hare that every so often turned up in the clearing in front of the house. Nonna Eia said she left a little present for me each time. I'd never seen her, but the presents were there. A small wooden box, a pen with an old-fashioned nib, a tiny mouse made of blue glass. All I had to do was dig alongside the prow of the broken-down boat.

When the cookies were finished, I ate all the anchovy quiche while Nonna watched. I didn't have the heart to bring it back home.

Then we went outside. I stuffed my nightgown back inside my jeans and started digging. I unearthed a conch shell, the spiral kind, and scraped off the dirt with my fingers. It was in perfect shape. Inside, it was a pale, delicate pink.

Back in the kitchen, I rinsed the shell to make it shine. Then I loosened the nightgown and let it fall back over my jeans, seized the flowers, nudged Nonna into a corner, and asked her to give me my cues.

"You're the king and you have to say, 'How do you, pretty lady?'"

"'How do you, pretty lady?'" asked Nonna Eia, putting on a manly voice.

"'Well! They say the owl was a baker's daughter. . . .'" I clutched the flowers tight in one hand and waved the shell around with the other. "'Lord . . . Lord . . .'"

"'Lord, we know what we are, but know not what we may be,'" the king prompted me.

I repeated the line with feeling and jumped ahead a little. "'There's rosemary, that's for remembrance.'" I was speaking the lines into the conch shell, which I held near my mouth like a microphone. An added touch.

"'And there is pansies, that's for thoughts. . . . There's fennel for you, and columbines. . . .'"

I kept going, getting more agitated. The conch shell bobbed up and down because I had to strew Nonna's flowers on the floor at the same time. I was Ophelia. I was a lost soul, out of my mind. "'And will he not come again?'" I crooned. "'And will he not come again? No, no, he is dead.'"

I was on the verge of tears. All at once I threw myself into Nonna's arms, even if that wasn't what Ophelia would do.

Nonna Eia applauded. "You're going to become a great actress, Elisa." Her eyes were glistening. "You were fantastic. I was a pretty good Ophelia when I was young, I've always had a weakness for that character. But you put something extra into it. It shows you really understand her. Give me another kiss. And now, do you feel like listening to your old grandmother?"

I said I'd love to.

Nonna Eia grabbed the teapot and pressed it to her chest, pretending it was Yorick's skull. Then she began Hamlet's monologue.

I listened with my mouth open.

Chapter Three

Back home, I went straight to my room to get rid of my big belly before Mamma got home from work. I didn't want her to know I'd gone out with my nightgown under my clothes.

Mamma didn't like anything the least bit out of the ordinary. No weirdness, no way. If I said something kooky, she'd give me a look, a worried little smile. And if I did anything unusual when she was around, like waving my arms around and making sneering faces in front of the mirror, she'd wrinkle up her brow and scrutinize me in silence, her eyes narrowed. If she happened to be busy with something in the house, she would gradually pretend to go back to whatever she was doing, but I could tell from her distracted, automatic movements that she was keeping an eye on me. So I'd quickly shape up and act normal.

I knew my mom was sad. Being widowed so young has to make women sad. I was a year old when my dad died. With so many photos of a man who was no longer with us scattered all over the place, the house felt too big. I felt as if those portraits gave off dark rays that faded the colors of the furniture, the walls, even our faces. My mom and I seemed like two silent fish crossing paths in an aquarium.

I took my time changing my clothes. Mamma's newsstand closed at seven-thirty; there was plenty of time before she came home.

In a vague, hazy way, I realized I had always known there was a mystery in our family. A skeleton in the closet, as the stories say. For a moment I fantasized about illegitimate children and secret pacts: Someone had forbidden Nonna ever to see her daughter again because . . . because if she did . . . then what? I couldn't imagine how the story would continue. I thought over all the questions Mamma would ask whenever I returned from visiting Nonna Eia. Was her house warm enough? Did she ever forget to turn off the gas on the stove? What was she wearing? Was she eating? What did she eat? Did she seem tired?

Until that day, I had always tried to answer with lots of details: When it's dark Nonna uses candles, she doesn't have electricity. It's to save money, though she likes beeswax candles, which are expensive. There's never even a crumb on the floor. She's always dressed in white, the cleanest color in the world. Her garden is beautiful, with all the vegetables she could want.

When I talked about Nonna, I could sense that I had Mamma's total attention. She practically hung on my words. And yet, I never told her about the canvases Nonna Eia had just finished working on in the shed. I don't mean the little pictures she still made every now and then for tourists. No, these new ones she kept for herself; she didn't want to sell them. There was something really strange about them, and I was afraid my mother would get alarmed if I described them.

That evening, after she put the soup on the table, Mamma began with her usual questions.

"How was Nonna today? Did she remember to go and cash her pension check?"

We were at it again!

"Nonna's just fine!" I burst out. "It's not like she's losing her memory!"

"A good thing too." A shaky smile. "It could be a problem if —"

"She's . . . she's perfectly capable of taking care of herself. Better than you or me. She doesn't need anyone's help." I realized how angry my voice sounded, as if it came from someone else.

"What is it? Did she say anything to you?" Mamma kept stirring her soup with a spoon. A lock of hair was nearly covering her eyes but she didn't make a move to brush it away.

Now I could see it: the SECRET. A big opaque bubble hanging between us in midair. It blocked our view. It prevented Mamma and me from looking each other in the eye. I opened my mouth to send out words as sharp as tacks. I had to burst that bubble as fast as I could.

"If you want to know how she is, Mamma, why don't you go see her? How come you never go? I mean, it's not like she lives at the North Pole!" I didn't raise my voice, but my tone was sharp and taunting.

Mamma stopped stirring the soup in her bowl. She was so stunned and upset and shamefaced and who knows what else — as if my tacks had pierced not the bubble-secret but my mother herself, straight through the heart. I had to look away.

"She told you." It wasn't a question. "Nonna told you all about it, right?" I heard her voice break. I couldn't bear it. I watched her look for her cigarettes and matches, light one, and take a greedy puff.

"No, Mamma. Nonna Eia said you're the one who should talk to me. She didn't want to eat the quiche because . . . because . . ."

"Because she thought I made it?" A whisper, without removing the cigarette from her lips.

"Yes."

Mamma started to cry. No sobs, just soundless tears that rolled slowly down her face, not like the torrents that gushed out when I cried.

I got up and went to slip in between her knees and give her a hug. Mamma was soothed almost right away and squeezed me tight. She moved the chair so I could sit on her lap the way I used to when I was little. Except when I was little I was the one crying, not her.

"I'm ten years old. I have a mind of my own. I can understand everything."

"I know." She squeezed me tight. "It's just that . . ." She cradled me in her arms and rocked me just a bit. "I should have told you about it long ago."

"So tell me now. Please." I waved my hand to get rid of the smoke.

She took a deep breath, like a diver getting ready to jump. "Elisa, you've always known your grandmother as calm and serene. But years ago, before you were born, one day, all of a sudden . . ."

I'd straightened up so I could look her in the face. She was speaking with her eyes closed, the cigarette between her fingers forgotten.

"Nonna Eia lived alone in the apartment below ours. We saw each other all the time, as you can imagine. Until one day . . . out of the blue . . . Well, she hadn't come upstairs for a few hours, so I went down to her. I found her standing absolutely still at the window, holding a teapot in her hand. She just stood there bewildered, staring at the teapot, so bewildered . . . as if she didn't know what it was. I spoke to her, but she didn't answer. She didn't recognize things anymore. Like, she picked up a shoe and didn't know what it was for. Or a chair. She was beyond all reason. It got worse each day. She saw things that weren't there. She didn't recognize people. She'd constantly be getting lost. We'd find her far from home, ready to drop from exhaustion. I wanted her to live with us, and we tried it for a while,

but your father didn't feel comfortable with that because . . .
she was becoming dangerous. Can you understand, Elisa?"

"Dangerous? How?"

"Dangerous to herself. She'd forget to turn off the faucets
and the apartment would be flooded. One morning she drank
a whole bottle of her cologne, 'Wild Breeze.' Afterward, she
gave off whiffs of perfume every time she opened her mouth."
Mamma stubbed out her cigarette on her plate.

"She still does."

"What?"

"Her breath smells of spices and jasmine."

"Even now? You never told me!"

"You never asked."

"Well, those weren't all the crazy dangerous things. Toward
the end she tried to do something dreadful. . . . We found her
leaning out over the balcony, waving her arms around like
wings. Do you see what I mean? I grabbed her just in time. We
couldn't keep her at home anymore, and she couldn't live alone
either. So I signed the papers."

"The papers?"

"The papers to have her admitted to an institution. I didn't
know what else to do."

"You mean a mental hospital? Nonna was in a mental
hospital?"

"It was the only place where she could get help. The doctors diagnosed schizophrenia. I went to visit her, but she refused to see me. If she so much as caught sight of me she'd fly into a rage. She knew I was the one who signed to have her admitted. And she knew that without my signature they couldn't keep her there."

"She didn't want to stay!"

"Right."

"But why did you have her locked up? Nonna's fine! I see her every day. She's not crazy!"

"Before she went to the hospital she was. They did something for her there, they cured her. She stayed almost four years. But after, when she was discharged, she wouldn't come back and live near us. Since she was the widow of a worker at the shipyard, the city gave her a house in Celestia. The house where she still lives. When I found out it was just a run-down shack, I tried to find a better place for her, but she refused. I had friends visit her, to make sure she was all right. She wouldn't speak to me. The doctors were mistaken in their diagnosis. It wasn't actually schizophrenia. Still, they warned me to be careful — she couldn't tolerate violent emotions. She could have a relapse."

"Is that why you never came with me?"

"I was afraid if she saw me, she'd get too upset. In the hospital she'd have a fit if she even spied me in the distance. But when you were born, I thought she might enjoy knowing her granddaughter. I named you Elisa because it has the same vowels as Eia, her name. I had friends take you there. Even when you were a tiny baby. Everyone told me how happy she was to see you. Meanwhile, I myself had to learn to live without her."

"Without your mamma," I murmured.

"Without my mamma."

My eyes were closed now too. I was feeling drowsy. I don't know how long we rocked each other without a word, and then Mamma broke the silence.

"It's very important that you visit her, don't you see? Not just because it gives her such pleasure. Thanks to you I can make sure she's okay, that nothing's starting to go wrong again. . . . Will you tell me, really, if you notice any odd behavior? You know, any peculiar signs . . . Will you be on the lookout?"

"Mm."

"Promise?"

I breathed out a grunt, "Umm."

I was doing something I'd never done in my entire life: I was pretending to fall fast asleep right there on her lap. I didn't want to answer. I didn't want to promise. It was as if Mamma was asking me to be a spy. To betray Nonna. She meant well, for sure, but something inside me rose up in protest.

Then I think I must have truly fallen asleep, because I woke up in my bed, under the covers, with the sun beaming in through the window.

Chapter Four

I was back again at the door with the peeling planks. Nonna Eia opened it, gave me a searching glance, and asked, "Where shall we go for our talk? It's too lovely a day to stay inside."

I agreed solemnly. I understood what she wanted to talk about. Wide open spaces, grand vistas — that was the proper stage setting for what Nonna was about to reveal.

"How about going to the Lido?" I suggested. It was a warm day in May; the ocean, it seemed to me, should be vast enough to keep our secrets.

"The Lido?" Her face lit up, and she put her hand to her head, as she did whenever she was excited. It was one of her typical gestures — she would crook her elbow and bring her hand to the top of her head, then hold her palm pressed there, as if to show how happy she was. But she let her arm fall and shook her head. "No, we can't. We'd spend too much time getting there. You have to be home by seven-thirty. What if we went to the top of the tower of San Marco?"

"But Nonna . . . there'll be so many tourists!"

"You're right. So where?"

Where? I bit my lips as I tried to think of someplace.

"What about this?" Nonna Eia proposed. "First, let's get away from here. Then I'll close my eyes and hold your hand. You'll lead me as if I were blind and describe everything you see. If you can make me so curious that I can't help opening my eyes, then it'll be my turn to be the guide, until I find someplace I like. Then I'll tell you to open your eyes and we'll stop. How do you like that game?"

I liked it and told her so. For a fleeting instant I wondered if Mamma would think that idea was an example of odd behavior.

When we'd gone far enough not to risk meeting anyone who knew us, Nonna closed her eyes. I held her left hand tight and told her to walk very close to me. Her hand was cold, her skin thick and coarse. Her steps were slow and heavy. I peered at her curiously. The wrinkles around her closed eyes seemed carved in an intense expression, and her lips were thrust forward, firm and concentrated. Her face looked naked and old and vulnerable.

I walked on the canal side, so she wouldn't be in any danger. I started describing the places we were passing. I was so caught up in my task that I forgot why we were looking for a quiet, open space.

"We're on a very narrow side street, very straight. I see a

yellow sheet hanging high up. A red tablecloth and white pajamas . . . an old woman watching us from her window . . . Now we're turning. . . . There's a well, a bench. . . . Now we're in a small square. . . . Now we're coming under a portico. . . . I see a porcupine. . . ."

"It must be part of a family coat of arms," Nonna murmured casually, without opening her eyes. "Under the portico. I remember that."

"There are two children . . . a gray cat . . . a closed window . . . and I see a pineapple!"

"A pineapple? There's no coat of arms with a pineapple!" Nonna stopped and opened her eyes.

We were right in front of a fruit stand.

"I made you look! Now it's my turn!"

I closed my eyes tight and felt my grandmother squeezing my fingers hard in her cold hand. "Ready?" she asked.

"Ready!" She'd never be able to make me open my eyes.

We walked along in silence for a minute or so. It was a strange feeling, moving in darkness as if I were blind. For the first few steps I was stiff as a puppet, glued to her side. Then I stopped trying to control things. Nonna wouldn't let me fall in a canal.

"A step up," she said. "Another. Another." I realized we were climbing onto a bridge. When we reached the top, she paused. I paused with her, keeping my eyes closed. "Look,

look," she said in surprise. "What could that be? In the canal, right under us — it looks like a big fish swimming underwater. Now it's leaping up! It's a dolphin!"

"No cheating, Nonna!" I giggled but kept my eyes shut.

"I forgot to tell you a very important rule of this game. The blind one can never challenge what the other person sees. No matter what it is, she has to believe it." She went on, a little faster.

"A step down. One more. One more." We were coming down from the bridge. She kept on enumerating arches, trees sprouting from walls, people, all kinds of shops.

"Now we've come to a field. There's a silken carpet spread on the ground. Very big, blue and gold. Now we're standing right on it!"

We had stopped. I hesitated and scraped my feet. I could feel something soft under my shoes. Could I really be walking on a silken carpet? I opened my eyes.

"It's a bath mat! It fell from that line up there!" I cried indignantly.

Nonna shrugged her shoulders.

"Now it's my turn!"

I realized how the game worked. We passed by canals covered with slabs of ice. Instead of laundry hanging on the lines, there were hundred-thousand *lire* bills. A lion cub was drinking from a well. Nonna Eia held out, asking for all the particulars, making me give more and more precise details, without ever opening her eyes.

After the umpteenth bridge I was starting to get tired. I'd just seen a gondola jam-packed with animals, like a small model of Noah's ark, sailing away on the canal. We were at San Pietro di Castello. There were some benches in the deserted space in front of the church. Without another word, I led Nonna over to one.

"You can open your eyes now," I announced and sat down.

Nonna Eia obeyed. She smiled at me. "Do you know what this game is called?"

"What?"

"Trust. Oh, look, here's a tortoiseshell comb." She bent down to pick up an old comb lying on the ground, nearly all its teeth missing. It had only the two biggest ones at the sides and one in the middle. She held it up vertically, with the three teeth facing east.

"It looks like an *E*," she remarked.

"The initial of our names."

"Just think, this comb was once part of a living being, some creature from who knows where." She stroked it gently, carefully rubbing it clean until the brown pattern shone under her fingers. "Who knows where . . ."

"Sit down, Nonna, please. We have to talk."

She obeyed as she slipped the toothless comb into the ample pocket of her white dress.

For a moment, we sat silently watching the boats moored in the canal in front of us: fishing boats with sails and big, flat-bottomed boats with the paint flaking off. No gondolas. The boats were rocking gently, their images reflected in the water. We were in the midst of a broad open space. Airy.

"Mamma told me about the mental hospital," I mumbled.

"It was so long ago." Nonna Eia looked straight ahead, her gaze lost in the canal and the wall opposite. "I never quite understood how it began . . . at what point I couldn't recognize things, and all the rest. I only know I was trying to transform myself so I wouldn't die. . . . I don't mean physical death — there are so many ways you can die, you know. . . . I can remember the motorboat as if it were yesterday — that was the ambulance that took me away. . . . I was screaming and struggling and my daughter stood right there watching!" She shook her head as if to drive away the image. "Life was dreadful in that hospital. They didn't want me to transform myself. Oh no! No transformations there. They forced me to turn back, to return to my old identity. I resisted at first, but then . . . It was all so cruel. Do you know what shock treatments are?"

I nodded in silence.

Nonna Eia took the comb from her pocket and started fiddling with it absentmindedly. "That wasn't the only thing. The doctors were so uncaring. . . . They spent so little time with the patients. It was ridiculous — two minutes per person and then on to the next. And the absurd restrictions . . . It was horrible. Horrible. Simply to get out of there I did whatever they wanted: I went back to what I was before."

She broke off. She was staring at the comb, but I knew she wasn't really seeing it. She was completely absorbed in the past. Then she must have remembered something that lightened her mood. She began speaking again.

"I had some friends in the hospital, other crazy people. Every one of them was seeking something. What is it Shakespeare says in *Hamlet*? 'We know what we are, but know not what we may be.' The people we call crazy are drifting in confusion, seeking what they might become. Can you understand that?"

I wasn't sure I understood, but I nodded anyway.

Nonna Eia returned to her story. "I lost all sense of time. I never knew if it was day or night. It didn't matter anyway. Finally, a doctor gave me some paints and I began making pictures. Not those saccharine little pictures I used to do. Up till then, in my previous life, I had just made paintings other people would like, to earn money. From that day on, I started to paint what I myself liked. So, you see, in a way that whole awful mess I got into, trying to transform myself — what the doctors called my madness — served some purpose after all.

But still, I can't forgive my daughter. No human being has the right to lock up a fellow creature. Never, no matter what the reason."

"Mamma was worried about you." I felt the need to justify my mother. I didn't like thinking of her in the role of torturer.

"For her, anything the least bit odd is dangerous. She'd have me locked up again today if she thought it was necessary. That's why I'd rather stay out of her way."

There was nothing I could say to that. I knew all too well that it was true.

"If I were ever put in a mental institution again, I think I'd give up the ghost in a couple of days." She said this calmly, like someone simply stating an absolute certainty, but I was caught short and didn't quite grasp the sense of her words. They echoed in my ears like sounds without meaning. I gave her a blank look.

"I would die," she whispered.

"But you'll never be locked up again," I cried, hugging her tight so she couldn't let out another word. I felt like Nonna Eia had said something monstrous. "You're not crazy!" With my face close to hers I could smell her spicy breath. I remembered the bottle of "Wild Breeze" cologne she downed years ago as if it were a soda.

"Oh no? Suppose I told you that under those boats I can see . . . giant jellyfish swimming around?"

"Where?"

"Down there . . . Oh, I can't see them anymore! They've gone down too deep. They're swallowed up!"

"I saw them! I got a glimpse of them just before they disappeared. . . . I saw them, Nonna!" I stretched my eyes as wide as I could, to make her think I was bursting with excitement. "Really! Really and truly! They were . . . they were bright blue, like iridescent jelly, with tentacles! I'm telling you, I really saw them!"

She gave me a big smacking kiss. "Thank you, Elisa." She sighed. "There is one thing I'm grateful to your mother for."

"What's that?"

"That she lets you come visit me."

Chapter Five

I remembered our game of Trust very well: It was the last time Nonna Eia seemed like her usual self.

It was awhile before I saw her again. Five days, if I remember right. The school year was almost over and the fifth-grade exams were coming up. Not that I was so worried, but the tense atmosphere that took over the class pressured me to study more than ever. I spent whole afternoons doing homework, either alone at home or at Francesca's house. When Saturday came at last, I went to Celestia.

I found Nonna in the shed, intent on her painting. She was using an old canvas; I recognized it because it was the largest one in the studio. It used to show two angels with goats' feet. It was a fun painting, kind of irreverent, but now the hooves, the wings, and everything else had disappeared under a layer of white paint. The canvas was set up on an improvised easel and Nonna Eia stood in front of it so that her back hid what she was painting.

"I thought you liked those goat-angels!" I exclaimed.

Nonna turned toward me. "Yes, but I needed a big canvas. And I was too impatient to go buy a new one."

She stepped aside so I could see her work.

It was a huge jumble of colors. Blue, dark red, yellow, black. And turquoise. No human figures.

"Are you getting into abstract painting?" I asked.

"Mm. It's not finished."

I stood watching her work for awhile. Bit by bit, every corner of the canvas was being covered by turquoise and violet. We were both very quiet. I knew from experience that Nonna didn't like to talk while she worked. I also knew that if I was there, in about ten minutes she would stop concentrating on her paintings and give me her full attention. So I waited.

She worked soberly, with leisurely gestures. She would dip the brush in the jar of turquoise, let it drip, and then, in no hurry, bring it to the canvas. She stood still for a moment, as if to decide which way to move her hand, then let the paint flow gradually over the surface, dragging the brush as if it weighed more than two hundred pounds. All her gestures were slow and deliberate.

About twenty minutes went by and Nonna still gave no sign of stopping.

"Nonna," I called at last, feeling bored. "I brought you some *zaeti*. I bought them. I had too much homework so I couldn't cook." I knew Nonna had a weakness for those biscotti to dip in sweet wine.

She roused herself. She had the same absorbed, vulnerable expression I'd noticed when she was walking with her eyes closed. She put the brush in the jar of turpentine and wiped her hands on a rag. "That's very sweet of you, Elisa."

Again I noticed how slowly she moved. It was like slow motion.

"This can wait," she said, with one last glance at her work. In those twenty minutes, she'd added some gray splotches to the turquoise parts of the picture. They looked weird, like mushrooms with lumps.

We went into the kitchen, and she made tea while I watched. I was a little disappointed that she didn't take out the bottle of dessert wine. Her gestures were sluggish, her back more bent than usual. She stood up chewing the biscotti for a long time, dipping them in the tea one by one. She ate greedily. It took forever.

Valentina, the hare, had brought me another gift: a tiny bracelet of beads, red as rubies. After I put it on my wrist, I recited the balcony scene from *Romeo and Juliet*. Nonna gave me the cues — her Romeo was young and fiery, full of passion, but I got mixed up because I hadn't had time to go over my lines.

Before I left I drew close to give her a kiss and noticed how wrinkled her neck was. Her skin was chilly and sagging; it drooped in folds and pouches under her chin. I'd never really stopped to think about old people's bodies and how relentlessly they waste away.

"How old are you, Nonna Eia?" I asked.

"Over eighty."

"That's not so old," I declared. "Francesca's nonna is ninety-four."

"Then I'm just a kid," she said ironically, putting a hand to her head. "I have my whole life ahead of me."

She held the door open as I left and watched me from the doorway. She'd taken the tortoiseshell comb from her pocket and with an idle gesture passed its three teeth through the white hair over her forehead. She smiled and said good-bye, waving her braid like a handkerchief.

The next Tuesday I found Nonna Eia in the shed again. She'd stacked all her old paintings on the empty fruit crates, with the picture sides toward the wall. She was using new canvases. The only painting in sight was the one she'd been working on the last time I was there. I went up close to see it better. It looked like a lunar landscape. Or Martian. Strange gray shapes in the form of mushroom clouds, on an unlikely turquoise sea. The sky was flecked with white dots. Seagulls?

"Is it done?" I asked.

"Mm. Maybe." She didn't even look up from her work. She

was busy stitching four canvases together to make one enormous one. The whole thing was propped up vertically, barely slanting, on a makeshift wooden trestle. It was so tall that Nonna couldn't reach the top part with her brush.

"Give me a hand," she said. "I have to spread this out on the ground."

After we moved some buckets, together we placed the gigantic picture on the ground, which was dotted here and there with blades of grass. For the moment, all she'd painted was a layer of turquoise and green with blotches. I couldn't make any sense of it: It wasn't pretty and it wasn't ugly.

Nonna crouched down alongside the painting and, with rather clumsy gestures, smoothed it out carefully, straightening the seams of the various canvases wherever the stitching was sloppy. Curled up on the ground like that, with her bent back sticking up, her white dress around her hips, and her massive legs folded under her, she looked huge. I had never thought of Nonna as fat. Stocky maybe, even solid and plump, okay — but not fat. But now there was something elephantine about her.

"What are those splotches?" I asked timidly.

"I don't know yet."

"You don't know what you're painting?"

"Not really. I'll find out as I go along. Do me a favor and pass me the paint jars. Put them here on the ground."

I took the jars, one by one, from where they were lined up on the crate and set them down on the dirt floor.

"You'll get your dress dirty, Nonna," I remarked.

"Oh, I'll be careful."

"Should I put the jar with the brushes down there too?"

"Sure."

She got back to work. Ignoring me.

I sat down beside her with my legs crossed and set about studying her.

The woolly white braid wasn't as thick as I remembered it, and it fell over one shoulder, covering her neck. I studied her arms. Her short-sleeved summer dress showed her forearms, but you could hardly make out her elbows, they were so rounded. Her wrists were like miniature tree trunks, broad and muscular. And her hands! Two paddles with short, thick fingers that could hardly manage to grasp the thin brush. Her nails were sturdy and square.

Next I studied her legs. They were shocking: thick and wide as elephants' legs, and the skin was grayish and scaly. Her upper body had gotten thicker too, and her back had a distinct curve that made it as round as a little hill. It must have been because of her position: Nonna had never been stooped over. In all that mass of flesh, her head seemed very tiny. I'm not sure why, but that in particular was what wrung my heart: the tiny little head and the long, thin, wrinkled neck. And her face too, all shriveled up, with bags under her eyes and heavy, drooping lids that gave her a sleepy look. She seemed terribly vulnerable. It made my head spin, seeing her like that.

I leaned forward to give her a hug.

My surprise embrace seemed to throw Nonna off balance. "Hey, hey." She let the brush drop so she could hug me back. I smelled her spicy breath, and the familiar aroma set things right again. The world fell back into place.

"Now we'll go for a walk. How's that?" She smiled. "I've been really selfish, painting all this time, while you're here. It's because . . . I don't know, lately I feel such pressure to finish this. . . ." She pointed to the canvas.

"Do you really not know what it'll turn out to be, Nonna?"

She laughed. "That's how it is. I don't have any plan. I'm just following the impulse of the moment."

"Is that a good way for a painter to work?"

"I don't know, Elisa. It feels right for me. It's like I'm chasing after a vision, but the vision itself isn't clear. I can't put it into words. That's why I have to paint it. But that's enough for now. Help me get up."

It was like trying to lift a huge sack of cement; it took all my strength to hoist her up. Luckily, Nonna Eia was laughing; otherwise it would have been pathetic.

When she was back on her feet, she stared down at the unfinished painting spread out on the ground. Her eyes, beneath the heavy lids, were tender. "Who knows what it is?" she murmured.

"But that one," I said, pointing to the canvas on top of the fruit crate, the one with the gray mushrooms. "You know what that one is, don't you?"

She turned to look at the painting. "Well, what do you see there?"

"Me? How should I know?"

"What do you mean, how should you know? What kind of answer is that? Come on, Elisa, use your imagination."

But for once I didn't have a ready reply. "Poisonous mushrooms?" I blurted out, just to say something.

Nonna burst out laughing and shook her head.

"I may not know what it is, but I'm sure it's nothing poisonous," she declared. "It's something exciting, don't you think?"

"Psychedelic mushrooms!"

She gave me an odd look. "I don't think they're mushrooms. It's . . . It's . . ." She stared off into the distance and said no more.

After that, I wasn't able to visit Nonna as often as usual because of exams coming up. Venice was sunk in a stifling heat wave, and my studying wore me out. Mamma thought I needed exercise, and decided to take me to the Lido with Francesca on Sunday — our first beach day of the season. This meant fewer visits to Celestia. While I splashed in the water — it was still pretty cold — and sprayed Francesca, or ran around on the sand enjoying the sunshine, I didn't think about Nonna. All I thought about was how I couldn't wait till school was over so I could go to the Lido every day.

More than a week went by before I saw Nonna again. And when I did, I wasn't prepared for the change.

Nonna Eia looked so much older. When I hugged her, her skin felt very rough. Her thick, coarse arms seemed to have scales instead of skin. They were tanned, but not in the usual way; it was as if a merciless sun had been constantly beating down on her. Her face was tanned too, but without the gold highlights that shone on mine.

"Nonna, are you okay?" I asked, stepping back.

"What did you say?"

I spoke louder. "Are you okay?"

"I've never been better."

And she gave a tranquil smile. She wasn't saying it to make me feel better, she really meant it. This was even more puzzling: How could she be okay if her eyelids were so puffed up that her eyes seemed to have shrunk in comparison, and her beautiful braid was reduced to a miserable little string? I could glimpse big bronze patches on her skull, where there was no hair left to cover it.

I didn't know how to broach the subject without hurting

her feelings. How could I tell her that she looked awful and seemed to be aging practically as I watched? Until that day I'd never had to repeat myself either. Was she getting deaf, besides?

"Come look at my paintings," she said abruptly. "I'm curious to know what you think."

We went into the shed. By this time all the canvases had been painted over. There was no trace left of the goat-angels and the mermaids. All the new pictures showed more or less the same thing: a hazy seascape with rocks shaped like mushrooms rising up from the turquoise water. The rocks were covered with a layer of low grayish-green shrubbery. I'd never seen anyplace like that. The biggest painting, the one made of the four canvases stitched together, was starting to look like the others — a harsh lunar landscape. The shapes weren't clear: dark, smooth, roundish masses, all crowded together under the usual mushrooms. What were they?

As I turned to ask her a question, I noticed something on the ground. A cabbage, partly chewed. What was it doing there on the dirt floor? Nonna followed my glance, observed the cabbage, but said nothing.

I restrained the urge to pick it up and turned back to the pictures. "Now do you know what you've been painting?" I asked warily.

"What?"

"Do you know what your paintings are?"

"Yes. Now I know."

I watched her carefully. She was standing up, bent over, with her glittering little eyes moving from one picture to another. I noticed that her irises had darkened from brown to a deep black. They seemed all pupil. I'd never heard anything about eyes darkening with age, but that's what it looked like.

"It's a place." She said it like that was all I needed to know, as if the word "place" explained everything.

"Yes, but what place?" I asked.

"An important place. I think I dreamed it."

"But were you ever there awake?"

"I don't know. . . . I don't think so. But still, I don't think I made it up. It has to be somewhere."

"Then it must have a name," I said.

"I don't know the name. I mean . . . I don't know the name in human language."

"How could that be? What other language could you know it in?"

"What was that?"

I said it again, louder. "Could you say the name in a non-human language?"

She smiled. Her rapid aging had dried up the fleshy part of her lips. They'd gotten so thin that you couldn't even see them.

"Do you want to hear it?"

"Yes."

She tossed her little head back. I say "tossed," but that's not quite the right word, because she did it very, very slowly, the way she did everything these days.

"Oorrsshhouffmmhh."

She said it in a wild, bold tone. Here again, the word "said" isn't quite right, because actually it was a sound, not a word. A thunderous sound, sort of like a roar. It had a kind of rumbling feeling, like sounds that come from the belly, but it also resonated like a joyous, irrepressible burst of life.

I'd never heard anything like it. I didn't know how to react so I burst out laughing.

I laughed as if it was funny, but actually I was getting rather uneasy. Nonna wasn't well, and I didn't know what to do. I had never seen her like this.

Should I tell Mamma?

However much she had aged, though, and however weird she had become, Nonna Eia hadn't lost any of her amazing intuition. Her glittering little eyes flashed at me as she said, "I don't know what language it is, and yet speaking it, I feel a new kind of happiness. I'm fine, Elisa. Truly. You don't need to worry about me." She picked up the cabbage from the ground, wiped it off on her dress, opened her mouth wide, and bit into it. "Mm. Delicious. I've found I really enjoy nibbling on raw greens while I paint. It makes me feel good, gives me energy. But don't tell your mother — she wouldn't approve."

Chapter Six

On the way home that day, I made up my mind to speak to Mamma. I was sure Nonna had to see a doctor right away. And yet when she asked me how Nonna was in that special anxious tone she had, I answered that she was just fine. Totally fine. At the last second, I mean literally the instant before I opened my mouth to speak, I changed my mind. I would try one last time to persuade Nonna to go to a doctor on her own, without anyone forcing her.

What I hadn't taken into account were my exams. For one whole week I was so caught up in anxiety and anticipation that my worry over Nonna Eia's health got shoved to the back of my mind, in a tiny dark corner where I completely lost sight of it.

But then, barely fifteen minutes after I realized I was done with elementary school forever — and that I had made my exit in triumph — I was overcome with guilt for forgetting all about Nonna. I decided to go see her right away, giving up the trip to the circus that Mamma was planning to celebrate my graduation.

I found Nonna in the shed, crouched on the ground. When I first glimpsed her from the doorway, I was blinded by the sun and didn't even recognize her. There'd been some drastic change.

The braid!

Nonna had cut it off. In its bare state, her head seemed even smaller. A few silver threads shone on her bronze skull.

And then, even before she turned to face me, I noticed another striking change.

She was painting with her hands. No more brushes! Nonna was dipping her fingers straight into the jars of acrylics and bringing them to the canvas on the ground, where she spread the colors in broad, trailing strokes. Like little children do with finger paints, the nontoxic kind you can lick.

"Nonna," I called in a low voice.

She turned slowly. At least she hadn't gotten any more deaf since last time. That was something!

"Hi, Elisa. So, did you pass all your exams?"

"Ye-e-s-s!"

I went closer and bent down to hug her. My sweet-as-sugar Nonna. Not a single spot on her white dress. How did she do it? Maybe it was because she moved like a Zen monk. Whatever it was, Nonna always looked spotless. I sat down beside her to look at the painting she was working on. More strangely shaped rocks.

"Now I know. It's an island," she said, before I could even ask. "But that's enough for today. We have to celebrate your graduation." She wiped her hands, which were spotted with turquoise and violet, on a rag and snatched up a carrot from the ground. "Want some?" she offered before she bit into it. I noticed something different in her mouth. I knew — because she'd told me herself, awhile ago — that she had worn dentures for years. But now I could have sworn she had something even more cumbersome in her mouth. I'd seen old people without their teeth: They looked awful, their lips all shrunken like a hen's butt. Well, Nonna Eia's mouth wasn't shrunken like a hen's butt. It was broad and protruding, no lips, hard as a bird's beak. And her nose? That was so flattened out that only the nostrils were visible above the thin mouth.

As if she could read my mind (more and more often, Nonna could guess what I didn't dare to ask), when she finished eating the carrot and swallowed noisily, she raised her head with a jerk and said, "The dentures were bothering me so I got rid of them. I can chew fine with my gums. It's lucky they've gotten so hard!" She chuckled contentedly, bringing her hand to her head. "I have to say that as time goes on I'm getting much tougher."

I helped her up; she seemed even heavier, and we could

hardly manage it. Back on her feet, Nonna Eia brushed herself off (if "brushed" is the right term for the maddening way she stroked the fabric of her dress, as if it were an antique tapestry) and smiled.

"I knew you'd be coming today, so I prepared something. Are you hungry?"

It was eleven in the morning and I wasn't hungry at all, but I lied just to make her happy. "Yes, I'm starved."

She laughed. "No, that's not true. You're not a good liar, Elisa. You're a good actress when it comes to Shakespeare, but in real life you don't know how to lie."

I thought how mistaken she was, considering all the things I hadn't told Mamma. Keeping quiet could be a kind of lying too: My silence was a lie.

"If you're not hungry, then let's take a walk!"

I agreed with relief.

Nonna walked down the street slowly on her short, heavy legs, one baby step after the other, and so bent over that the distance between her chin and the pavement was no more than a couple of feet. Strange that the weight of her head didn't drag her down to the ground! It must have been because it was so tiny that it didn't even yield to the force of gravity. I walked alongside her, purposely not helping so as not to embarrass her. I remembered that on our other walk, when we had had such fun playing at being blind, I hadn't noticed anything unusual except maybe her cold hands. But she certainly hadn't walked as if she were underwater! It was all happening so fast. What kind of sickness could it be? I thought of Methuselah from the Bible, the man who lived to be nearly a thousand years old. Was there some disease called Methusalitis?

It took us half an hour to get across the footbridge.

"Should we take the vaporetto?" I asked. I could see the water bus heading toward the pier.

"Yes. I have a yen for wind and sea. And then, Elisa, how about going to celebrate your graduation at Burano?"

I loved that idea. I'd always liked Burano, with its pastel-colored cottages, but actually what I liked even better was not having to walk alongside her in that spooky area near her house, terrified of meeting someone we knew.

Nonna bought the tickets, and we got on the vaporetto. At the *Fondamenta Nuove* stop we had to get off to change. But that wasn't a problem: It was late morning and there was plenty of time before I had to go home. We had the whole day ahead of us.

On the vaporetto we stayed outside, standing up, with the wind lashing our faces and the seagulls flying around. I cast furtive glances at Nonna. She was leaning her elbows on the railing, taking in noisy breaths of air, her eyes half closed. Her expression was happy and she exuded a sense of energy: Even though she seemed decrepit, she didn't look frail. She gave the impression of carrying herself with great dignity — her long, dark wrinkled neck, her columnlike arms, and her bent back — as if she were decked out in weighty, sumptuous formal dress.

"Nonna, do you ever go to the doctor?" I said casually, as if the idea had just been blown to me on the wind buffeting my face.

"What?"

"The doctor. Do you ever go?" I shouted.

With a start, she drew her head in toward her shoulders. "Why should I? Doctors are for when you're sick, and I'm never sick."

"At school they told us about preventive medicine. To make sure you don't get sick in the future."

Her neck gradually stretched out again and she laughed. "I won't get sick, rest assured, Elisa." She patted my hand, resting on the railing. "I wouldn't see a doctor for anything in the world. They don't understand a thing, those doctors."

I gave up with a sigh. I'd never seriously thought I could convince her anyhow.

At Burano, Nonna bought me a big, embroidered lace collar, all white and frothy. It reminded me of the costumes Shakespeare's characters wore.

We bought lettuce sandwiches and headed toward a small square surrounded by pale green, pink, and canary-yellow houses. We sat down on a bench in the sun, facing some trees.

After she ate her sandwich, Nonna Eia dozed off. That gave me an opportunity to take a good look at her without her noticing. As she slept, her long neck, which was slightly sunk in her shoulders, rocked back and forth with the rhythm of her breathing. Her little head nodded faintly. Up close, her head wasn't smooth; it seemed to be covered with a scaly bronze glaze, not very nice to look at. Once again, it wrung my heart. Once again, sitting in silence beside her on the bench, I decided that that very evening I would speak to Mamma. It was the only right thing to do.

I got home before seven and went to find Mamma. She was watering the plants on the balcony.

"Well, how was your day, Elisa? Did Nonna celebrate with you?"

"She sure did!"

Mamma kept on pouring from the little watering can she held in one hand. In the other she held a cigarette. "I was thinking how great it would be if you and I could take a vacation at the seashore this summer. Someplace far away, maybe Liguria. Or in the mountains . . . The only thing is, I don't have the heart to leave Nonna all alone — she's too old. If something happened while we were away . . . I'd never forgive myself."

"You're right," I murmured. "Nonna needs me. I think that . . . I think . . ."

This time I wouldn't hold back. I was about to launch into a description of all Nonna's problems and changes, but just at that moment Mamma put the watering can down under the running faucet, took a few puffs of her cigarette, and as she waited for the can to fill up, started talking in that determined tone people have when they've prepared their speech in advance.

"We'll take a vacation, Elisa, I promise, only not this year. Later on we'll be able to go. You see, I've been thinking a whole lot about how to deal with the problem of Nonna. She's getting old. Soon she won't be able to take care of herself anymore. It happens to all old people, even those who haven't had a history of . . . of emotional disorders. And since she's so stubborn about not wanting to live with us no matter what, I've been thinking about what kind of place would be right for her."

I listened with my heart in my throat. I had an inkling of what she was about to say.

Mamma raised the filled watering can and turned off the faucet. "Nowadays," she went on, staring straight at the plants she was back to watering, "there are beautiful places for old people. Real resort-type places, out in the countryside, far from the noise and bustle, where they're cared for day and night. They cost an arm and a leg, but I'm prepared to make any sacrifice for her. And then there's her pension, which would help us pay the expenses. I've found one, not far from Venice but farther inland. . . . It's really great. Believe me, I'd even live there myself!"

"But Nonna Eia would never want to leave her cottage in Celestia!" I protested softly.

"Yes, I suppose she's just as stubborn as ever. But she'll have to be convinced. Pretty soon it'll be too dangerous for her to live alone . . . especially in that hovel they gave her for a house!"

"But Nonna's still strong! She does everything on her own!"

"Yes, but . . . for how much longer? Sometimes old people fall apart all at once, you know."

"And if she won't be convinced?" I asked, trying to keep my lips from trembling.

"She's got to be convinced," Mamma retorted in a low voice, "and you can help me with that." The vase of geraniums was overflowing but she didn't seem to notice. She kept the watering can tilted even though it was totally empty. "I made a reservation for her and put down a big deposit. The place is called Villa Serena. They told me they'll have a vacancy in less than six months — she'll have to go or else we'll lose it. So we have almost six months to make her see that this is the best solution. I'm counting on you. She might listen to you. But no more depressing topics: Today you're the guest of honor. It's not every day that my favorite daughter graduates to junior high! How would you like to go out to the pizzeria?"

Calling me her "favorite daughter" was Mamma's affectionate way of teasing, seeing as I was her only child. The only joke she ever permitted herself, as far as I noticed.

I ate pizza that night without my usual eagerness. I kept thinking of Nonna Eia locked up in a rest home with other old people. Wouldn't it remind her of the mental hospital? Nonna didn't like to feel closed in, she didn't like being told what to do, she didn't like schedules. No, as long as I was around, Nonna wouldn't end up in an old people's home. All at once her condition struck me as much less serious than I'd been assuming lately. So what if she was losing her hair, or her skin was getting strangely darker, or she threw away her dentures, or she walked in slow motion? No, Nonna had to keep living however she liked. In her cottage. Because it truly was a cottage, not a hovel. I would look after her. I would manage everything. No one would make her do anything against her will — over my dead body.

As the pizza gradually disappeared into my stomach without my even tasting it, I planned my strategy. I would present a picture of Nonna as so sturdy, so self-assured, so capable of managing on her own, that Mamma herself would come to the conclusion that such a staunch old woman didn't need any nursing home. Then if Nonna ever needed help I'd be there to do everything. I would protect her from everything and everyone. Forever.

I swallowed the last mouthful of pizza and made my first move.

"Look what Nonna Eia just made me!" I exclaimed, and pulled a small package out of my jeans pocket. Luckily, there was no writing on the pale-blue wrapping paper. I showed Mamma the embroidered collar.

"You mean to say she made that? Impossible!"

"She just finished it today. She was working on it while I kept her company." Nonna, Nonna, how could you say I don't know how to lie?

My mother put aside her cigarette to snatch up the delicate lacework. She turned it over and over between her fingers, then brought it near her face to look more closely. "This collar is amazing. It could have been done by a professional! Such fine work . . . I didn't think she could still see so well at her age!"

"She certainly can. She can see better than you and me put together!"

From the astonishment on Mamma's face, I could tell I had won the first round.

After our trip to Burano, it was impossible to go out with Nonna Eia anymore.

It wasn't just that we were keeping track of the inches we covered instead of the yards. People were turning around to look at her. Nonna kept getting darker and heavier. And more bent over — her spine, by this point, was parallel to the pavement. Aside from that and her eerie slowness, though, she seemed fine. She took deep breaths and smiled a lot. Being so slow didn't bother her.

Still, Nonna Eia had noticed the curiosity she aroused lately when she was out walking, so she left the house only to walk in the garden and the meadow, where the dense shrubbery shielded her from inquisitive glances.

I realized she'd also become a vegetarian, so I stopped bringing her sardines marinated Venetian style and other meat or fish dishes. I picked wild cherries for her — she was even more of a glutton for them than I was. These days she was eating mostly raw fruit and vegetables. Aside from the sun, could that be why her complexion was so dark?

Often she would eat carrots from the garden, right out of the ground. She was content simply to wipe them off on her dress, which, sad to say, wasn't as white as it used to be.

I began going to the post office to cash her pension checks. Nonna had given me a written proxy; the clerk showed some surprise the first day, but after that, things always went smoothly. I used the pension money to do her shopping and all her other errands. I cleaned the house. I did the laundry. Sometimes a neighbor would stop me to ask how Nonna was and why she never went out walking anymore. "She's fine," I'd answer. "She's been busy. She doesn't want to be disturbed because she's painting." Then I would dash off. Fortunately, Nonna had never gotten too friendly with anyone in the neighborhood.

As far as Mamma . . . I knew a lace collar wasn't nearly enough to buy Nonna's freedom. Luckily, my piggy bank was really full. I bought other bits of embroidery, plus Venetian Carnival masks and fancy cookies and small watercolors, all of them "straight from Nonna's hands," to display to Mamma as signs of her total competence and independence. Mamma's eyes widened in puzzlement and wonder, and not once, all summer long, did she ever mention Villa Serena again.

Chapter Seven

Mamma and I didn't stir from Venice all summer. The city was wrapped in a muggy, torrid heat wave. Dense crowds of exhausted-looking tourists invaded the streets, making them impassable. Strange odors swept in from the canals in gusts, and the sticky air was filled with the Neapolitan songs of gondoliers gliding by under the bridges, their boats full of Japanese sightseers.

Nearly every day I went over to Nonna Eia's in the late afternoon, after I got back from the Lido, my fingertips white and shriveled from staying in the water too long.

I almost always found Nonna Eia in the shed, crouched down on the floor over her canvases. She painted like a demon the entire summer, as if her life depended on it. And the paintings were getting bigger all the time: I'd used her pension money to buy new canvases — I was saving mine to get some really fine handicrafts. All of Nonna's paintings showed seascapes, all of them very similar. The main colors were still blue, turquoise, and gray. There were no human figures or animals, except for a few birds in flight. Often the mushrooms that surged up from the sea were doubled, as if mirrored by the water they rose from. Several of the paintings featured mysterious dark, rounded shapes. Sometimes these fantastic scenes were lit by a single red flame.

"What island is that, Nonna?" I asked. "Do you know yet?"

"Al-da-bra," she answered, placing her hand on her head and chuckling, as if it were a magic spell invented on the spur of the moment. She spoke in such a low murmur that I was never sure I had understood right. I thought it might be her way of saying, "Who knows?"

One afternoon — it was already September — I couldn't find Nonna Eia anywhere. She wasn't in the shed, she wasn't in the garden, she wasn't in the house. It was unlikely that she would wander far from Celestia all by herself. Where could she have gone?

I roamed around outside the house calling her, then went in for a glass of water. In the kitchen, which was deserted and in perfect order (except for a few half-eaten lettuce leaves on the floor), I heard a faint noise coming from the bedroom. I headed in that direction, but the room was empty.

"Nonna?" I called softly from the doorway, a little bit frightened.

Again I heard the faint noise, like a scraping sound.

I looked at the bed — the sound seemed to be coming

from there. It was an ancient wooden bed, so high that I had trouble scrambling up onto it. Could there be a stray cat hiding underneath?

I went closer and bent down to look.

"Nonna!"

There she was. All curled up in a big ball. She must have fallen asleep under the bed and was just waking up. Her long dress, a cloudy gray now, was crumpled up and twisted clumsily around her body so that her thick legs stuck out. Even in the dim light under the bed, I could see how coarse and dark they'd become.

"Nonna, why are you sleeping under the bed?" I asked stupidly.

"It's so cozy here," she muttered in a low voice, showing no sign of wanting to move from the spot. I could barely make out her words in that hoarse whisper.

I bit my lips, wondering if it was really sensible to keep protecting my grandmother, hiding her peculiar habits from prying eyes. What was I doing? Why didn't I rush to tell Mamma?

Instead, I said, "Can I come down there with you?" Without waiting for an answer, I slid under the high springs of the bed frame, alongside her. I hugged her close, without a word. Nonna put her right arm around my waist.

"It's like a little house," I murmured after a long silence.

"What?"

"A little house."

"So it is. It feels safe, doesn't it?" Nonna's voice wasn't just low. It was thick and raspy, hardly understandable.

"But sooner or later we'll have to go out."

"Why?"

"To eat!"

We were whispering like two little girls playing a trick on the grown-ups.

At last, Nonna began to move out from under the bed on all fours. It took her forever, and when the process was completed, I slid out too. I straightened up and helped her get up from the floor. Later on, I made her take off her dress so I could wash it, but she wouldn't put on a fresh one; she preferred to wait wrapped in a sheet. Then when the dress was dry, she didn't want to put it back on. She said she preferred the sheet.

From that day on, whenever I didn't find her walking around I looked under the bed. For reasons I never quite grasped, that had become her favorite place to curl up for a nap. Not on the bed but under it, where she felt protected.

I tried to set my mind at ease: After all, I told myself, Nonna's little quirks were utterly harmless. Why waste time and energy struggling against her preference for sheets? But when I noticed that her fingers had gotten so thick that she couldn't hold on to things any longer, I suggested she see a doctor. Someone of her choice. "It could be a form of arthritis," I said. "Arthritis can be treated!"

"But I'm not in any pain, and I'm comfortable crawling on all fours! Now that I'm heavier, it's much more convenient," she replied in her raspy voice. "I don't need a brush for my paintings. I can do much better with my fingers. And I can still get my food to my mouth. Those are the only things that matter!"

"You can get it to your mouth, but not with a knife and fork."

"Well, so what?"

"And I'm the one who has to screw on the caps of the paints so they don't dry out. You always leave them open."

"I know you like doing it. I'm happy as I am, Elisa. I told you, doctors frighten me. They want everything their way, and I can't stand the way they tell you what's 'normal' and what's not. They think they know what's good for you, but actually . . ." She let out a hoarse, angry, incomprehensible hissing sound.

I could see there was nothing to be done. It was better to let it go. I had no one I could turn to for advice. If I told Mamma even a tiny fraction of Nonna's weird habits, she'd have her locked up straightaway. If I consulted a doctor . . . assuming I could find the right one (Francesca's uncle, for example, was a pediatrician), what would I say to him? "Listen, Doctor, my grandmother is changing into something not quite human . . . so far, I'm not sure what. She's turned a kind of bronze color, she crawls on all fours, she eats raw cabbage, and one day I saw her drinking from the basin and snorting the water in through her nose." For sure, Francesca's uncle would have *me* taken away in a water ambulance! I told myself that as long as I was with her, Nonna wasn't in any danger. But the minute she started complaining, or at the first sign of any pain, even minor pain, I'd hurry up and tell someone right away.

It wasn't until the day before school started that I realized what Nonna Eia had turned into. It came to me when I entered the shed and saw that she'd gotten rid of the sheet she hadn't parted with since she gave up regular clothes.

Nonna Eia was painting naked, crouched over the ground as usual. But the term "naked" doesn't really do justice to what I saw, because there's no way you can use the word "naked" for an enormous land tortoise. Strictly speaking, there's not a creature in the world that's less naked.

Only then, without the sheet covering her, did I notice the shell that had grown on Nonna's back: a true carapace with big gray plates. Later, when I stroked it, I felt how hard it was. At this point, not even in your wildest dreams would you say the huge paws protruding from it were legs. The same was true of her arms, which had no wrists and ended in five rough outlines of fingers with astonishing claws. As far as the head and the snout . . . there was no doubt they belonged to a huge tortoise. No nose, glittery beady black eyes, the jaws an opening halfway between a beak and a lipless mouth, the skin covered with wrinkles. Only a girl as clueless as I was could have taken so long to grasp the true nature of this transformation.

My grandmother was a little less than three feet tall and at least four feet long. The broad plates of her shell were pentagonal in shape, slightly rounded in the center, and separated from one another by thin white lines that might have been drawn by a very delicate brush. The plates of the lower section of the shell were narrower, and at the point where her neck emerged, they curled slightly outward. Near the tail, though, they bent modestly downward. The thick paws were covered with pentagonal scales as well. Her neck was long and her head could retract until it disappeared into the shell. Needless to say, I couldn't see her stomach, because Nonna couldn't stand upright anymore, not even with my help.

I wanted to find out exactly what Nonna Eia had become. And I wanted to know if there were other creatures like her in nature. I had a small computer at home that Mamma had given me for my tenth birthday, so I decided to begin my research there. At school they'd taught us how to use the Web. I logged on and started by typing in "tortoise." I searched for more than an hour. By the end I had located two kinds of tortoise that fit Nonna's description: the giant tortoise of the Galápagos Islands and the very similar one of Aldabra.

Aldabra! Wasn't that the word Nonna had muttered? She'd said something like Al-da-bra, and I thought it was some kind of magic spell. Maybe it was. Maybe the word itself had transformed her. . . . On second thought, no. The transformation had begun earlier. Quite a while earlier.

I typed in "Aldabra" and found the site.

There was a photo taken from the air. I clicked to maximize it and saw the islets of Aldabra surrounding an oval-shaped lagoon.

In another photo, I recognized Nonna Eia's mushrooms. They were coral reefs rising from the depths of the sea like spires, worn away by water at the base.

Next, I began reading. Aldabra is part of the Seychelle Islands, a remote atoll in the Indian Ocean. It was the world's biggest atoll of volcanic origin. I read that it had become a sanctuary, a protected refuge for the tortoises of Aldabra, which were an endangered species. *Geochelone gigantea* was the name of this prehistoric creature that had roamed the earth even before the dinosaurs.

At that point I typed in "*Geochelone gigantea*" and found tons of stuff in English. I got out my dictionary and began patiently translating it. These tortoises have a long, retractable neck that helps them look for food, and their limbs — also retractable — are shaped like elephants' feet, wider at the base. I kept reading, growing more and more excited. The males can weigh as much as six hundred and fifty pounds, the females a bit less. Some specimens live to be two hundred years old. They're herbivorous animals, and since their food can't run away, they don't have to move quickly. Besides, the adults have no natural predators, so there's no reason to flee. If need be, they can feed on dead carcasses, and they wouldn't turn down those of their own species either.

I was breathless: Everything fit together! Nonna — who knows why? — had become a *Geochelone gigantea*. For how long, I had no idea, but I suspected it might be forever.

I logged off and shut down the computer, even though my search wasn't finished. I'd had it for now; my head was spinning. I needed to think. How could this have happened? And why? Maybe I could learn something by questioning Nonna. While it was still possible to do that, for already her voice was a raucous hiss, the words all jumbled together. But I had no choice except to go to her and ask, "Nonna, why did you turn into a giant tortoise?"

Chapter Eight

When I got to Celestia, the tortoise was in the garden, so engrossed in her cabbages that she didn't even notice I was there. She was yanking them straight out of the ground with her mouth, not using her paws anymore. She would shred a chunk of cabbage with her sharp jaws, then raise her head high up and snap it back with a jerk — the only swift movement she could make — and swallow it in one lump. I could see the mouthful inside her neck — a little bulge making its way down.

I went closer and greeted her cheerfully, as if it were the most natural thing in the world to find your grandmother nibbling on cabbages.

Before I could reach her, she turned and stretched her neck toward me. Her massive paws straightened and rose, and the heavy shell began ascending in one uninterrupted, perfectly vertical motion that reminded me of the smooth precision of an elevator.

When she had stabilized at her full height, she started advancing toward me rather regally, narrowed her eyes, and said something.

I realized with horror that her voice was no longer the slightest bit human. I couldn't understand her.

"What did you say?" I asked, taking a step in her direction.

"Uh to arfe," Nonna mumbled, still upright on all four paws.

I went over to her, trying to hide my bewilderment. I stroked her neck. The skin was flaccid, neither hot nor cold. But I could smell her breath perfumed with jasmine, and that calmed me down.

"Nonna, I can't catch what you're saying. Could you write on the ground?" I hoped she could understand me, at least. She gazed at me, a baffled look in her liquid eyes. I repeated my question louder, recalling that she'd also grown slightly deaf lately.

This time she seemed to grasp what I was saying. She moved off, trying to find a patch of ground without any grass. I followed her slow steps. When she found a stretch of bare earth she bent over, putting the whole weight of her carapace on the ground to keep her paws free, and started scraping with the huge claws of her right paw. It took an eternity, partly because the ground wasn't perfectly level. I leaned over, waiting to see what would appear.

"That's a capital *C*, right?" I asked.

She nodded, her little head turned to me, then went on with her work.

After a quarter of an hour, I was able to make out "CIAO ELISA." The letters were all lopsided, but legible.

"*Ciao*, Nonna," I said, bending over to hug her long serpent's neck. It still took some effort to touch that unfamiliar skin that didn't feel like real skin. In a remote corner of my heart I harbored the absurd hope that a kiss would transform her back into a human being, the way the frog in the fairy tale was transformed into a handsome prince. It would be enough for me if she changed back into my grandmother. But that didn't happen.

The tortoise drew in her neck and let out a long puff of air, like a snort. It was the first time I'd heard her do that. It sounded like one of those blasts that erupt from the ocean when a great wave breaks like a geyser from a hollow in the rocks, with a din like a raging dragon. That was it — the sound Nonna Eia made was like an ocean whirlpool, a deep, prolonged *v-o-o-f-f*.

"You could use your paints to write on paper, but it would take too many sheets," I said, trying to hide my frustration. "It would be easier to use sand. Tomorrow's Sunday. I'll bring you some sand from the Lido."

"GOOD IDEA," she wrote. That took twenty minutes. When she was done, she cast me something like a smile.

"How are you feeling?" I asked.

"JUST FINE," was the answer, in block letters.

The following day I did what I said I would. I pestered Mamma to go back to the Lido, where I filled two plastic bags with clean sand. The bags were so heavy that if I'd added one extra grain I couldn't have hauled them back home.

"What do you want with all that sand?" Mamma asked.

"It's for Nonna. I think she wants to make a miniature Japanese garden. You know, the kind with stones and raked sand."

Mamma blinked. "Nonna Eia never ceases to amaze me."

"I know, she's so creative, isn't she?" I said brightly.

"She sure is!"

I carried the bags to Nonna's house that same evening, one in each hand, tottering under the strain of all that weight. When I got there I greeted the tortoise, who was painting in her studio, daubing on the colors with her thick paws.

I decided to spread the sand inside the shed. First, to be sure it wouldn't get scattered all over the ground and be wasted, I built a low border out of some old planks, making an enclosed area where I could pour the sand. The whole time I was busy with this project, the tortoise, who'd left off painting, watched attentively by my side, ready to give advice in her own way — by nudging my hand slightly up or down with her snout, for instance, so I wouldn't hit any knots in the wood as

I hammered in the nails. When the enclosure was ready, I emptied the two bags of sand into it, then flattened it out thoroughly with my hand.

"Okay, that's done. Now write something," I said.

The tortoise set to work in a hurry (in a manner of speaking, I mean). This time she wrote with her snout instead of a paw. She used her long flexible neck like an arm. Her beak left a clear mark in the soft, smooth sand. The whole operation went much faster than it had in the dirt patch of the garden.

"I LOVE YOU," she wrote. "DO YOU FEEL LIKE RECITING OPHELIA'S LINES FOR ME?"

"Yes, but who'll give me the cues?" I crossed out my writing and smoothed the sand down again to make room for her answer, because her capital letters were really huge.

"I WILL. I CAN SAY THE LINES TOO."

To tell the truth, nothing had really changed. I played Ophelia and Hamlet's voice came from Nonna's throat, mangled beyond recognition, but I knew the lines by heart now, so what difference did it make, as long as the tones and rhythms were right? When she did the part of Polonius her tone changed — it became unctuous, full of secret scheming.

I felt so relieved. As long as the tortoise still had Nonna Eia's brains and talent, nothing else really mattered.

I erased the writing again and asked as loudly and clearly as I could, "Nonna, why did you change into a tortoise? Do you know that you're a *Geochelone gigantea* from the Seychelle Islands? How come?"

"I DON'T KNOW. MAYBE THE TORTOISESHELL COMB HAD SOMETHING TO DO WITH IT," came the answer.

That toothless comb that she found near the park bench! If that was what had transformed Nonna, maybe it also had the power to undo the spell. I was even more relieved to know there was some reason for what had happened, a starting point. Whatever has a beginning has to have an end too.

"Is it magic?" I asked anxiously.

"I DON'T THINK SO. BUT IT MADE ME THINK ABOUT TORTOISES. I'VE BEEN THINKING ABOUT THEM EVER SINCE."

"And thinking about tortoises made you turn into one?"

"IT WAS A SPECIAL KIND OF THINKING. VERY INTENSE. SO INTENSE I DIDN'T EVEN KNOW I WAS THINKING."

"Oh."

So the comb wasn't magic after all. It had just given her the idea, the starting point for this new metamorphosis. The initial inspiration. But the power to transform — that Nonna had drawn from deep within, from her innermost self. Despite my disappointment, I still wanted to find the comb that had triggered everything.

"Where do you keep it?" I asked.

"I THINK IT WOUND UP UNDER THE BED."

I went to get it, then returned to the shed. I turned it over in my hands. A broken, useless, pathetic thing.

"Could you ever go back to what you were before, Nonna?"

"WHAT?"

I used the flat part of the comb to erase the writing in the sand and repeated in a very loud voice, "Could you become a woman again?"

"I DON'T WANT TO BE A WOMAN AGAIN. MY MIND IS AT PEACE NOW. I LIKE IT THIS WAY."

"But . . . what does it feel like?"

"IT'S HARD TO SAY. I FEEL PUSHED TOWARD THE DEPTHS AND THAT'S WHERE I DRAW MY STRENGTH."

"From the earth?"

"YES, FROM THE EARTH. A LOT OF ENERGY FLOWS INTO ME. I COULD HOLD UP THE WHOLE WORLD."

She drew a picture to illustrate her idea: a smiling tortoise with a ball poised on its back. That ball was the world.

She waited until I had smoothed out the sand again, then wrote, "AND I'M SO YOUNG NOW!"

I thought of the *Geochelone gigantea* that could live for two hundred years. Nonna was eighty: As a tortoise, she was a young girl! Well, not quite a girl, but she still had a whole life-time ahead of her.

With a sigh, I erased the writing with the comb. "But could you ever possibly go back to what you were?"

She tossed her little head and gave out one of her profound snorts. She seemed to be running out of patience with my asking over and over — but maybe that was just my impression.

At home, after I showed Mamma a red cotton beret "that Nonna Eia crocheted in two days" (it actually cost my whole weekly allowance), I shut myself up in my room to keep searching the Web. I wanted more information about the *Geochelone*.

I read about their habits. For example, they can drink through their nostrils. I remembered seeing Nonna Eia do that before her transformation was quite complete. And they remain fertile till they're very old. So Nonna might even give birth to babies, if only she could find a male of her species! All those little tortoises would be my aunts and uncles.

My reading turned up some really wild facts. When a female digs a hole to deposit her eggs, she urinates in it first — a lot — to soften the earth. I pictured Nonna doing that. It's weird how animals don't feel the least bit self-conscious even when they're performing the most private acts. I also learned that the oldest living tortoise in the world was two centuries old, was called Esmerelda, and was a male.

I continued searching the Web until I came across an animal-lovers newsgroup.

At school, I was good on the Web and had already tried joining newsgroups, but only the ones for rock fans. So I had no trouble introducing myself. I typed in my question.

"Is anyone interested in giant tortoises? Specifically, does anyone know anything about the *Geochelone gigantea* from Aldabra?" Since I was protected by anonymity, I didn't think I was taking any risks if I signed my first name.

Two hours later, when I checked to see if anyone had read my message, I found an e-mail in Italian from someone called Max.

"Hi, Elisa, why do you need information on the tortoise from Aldabra? I've been trying to buy one for years for my personal zoo. I should inform you that I have a reptile collection. Just reptiles. Crocodiles, snakes, iguanas, giant monitor lizards. I already have thirty species of land and sea tortoises, but I'm missing the queen of tortoises. So far I haven't been able to find any."

"Why do you collect only reptiles?" I asked, curious. Before I revealed that I had a giant tortoise from Aldabra, I wanted to know something about this Max character.

Pretty soon a very weird answer came back. "Haven't you ever collected anything, Elisa? The collecting urge comes from a need for completeness. I started when I was a kid, collecting live lizards. No spiders or ants. Only lizards. That's how it began. You get hung up on a certain kind of creature, and you want to possess it in all the various forms nature can offer. If you possess them all, then you control them. A specimen for every gradation of color, every tiny difference. If you're missing a single example of that species, you want it so badly you can go nuts over it. You become an expert. At a certain point you realize you've got almost all of them, and then you broaden your range, just a little bit; you branch out to similar varieties. That's how I got into other kinds of reptiles — to find the differences and similarities and where they overlap. To expand and complete the collection until it reaches the point of total inclusiveness. Only then can I rest. That, Elisa, is the path to happiness."

"I've never collected anything," I wrote back, confused. "Not even plastic figurines . . . But I would like to find out more about the *Geochelone gigantea*." I was seized by the urge to confide in someone, to tell a little bit of my secret. He didn't know who I was, after all. There was no danger.

"Because I have one," I added right before I sent my message.

I waited a day, then I found: "Elisa, that can't be. Who are you? A scholar? A scientist?"

"I'm ten years old," I confessed, because I knew that if he asked me any questions I wouldn't be able to pass myself off as a scientist.

An hour later a message arrived: "A kid! So you must have a small tortoise, maybe a radial turtle or a yellow mud tortoise, but not a *Geochelone gigantea!*"

"I really have a *Geochelone* from Aldabra, a huge one. About four feet tall and more than three feet long. I don't know how much it weighs, but it must be close to three hundred pounds," I typed.

"Tell me what it's like!" was the answer I received just a little later.

I realized he still didn't believe me, so I launched into a thorough description of Nonna Eia's physical traits and habits. I didn't omit the slightest detail except, of course, everything relating to her life as a human being.

"Assuming you're telling the truth, how'd you get it?" Max wrote back, losing no time. He was obviously sitting at his computer, same as I was.

"I found it."

"Where? That's impossible!"

"I found it not far from home," I typed in, getting a bit worried at the turn our correspondence was taking.

"If that's so, it could only have escaped from a zoo."

"Yes, that must be it. In fact, I'm sure of it."

"That's simply incredible! What zoo do you live near? Can I come see it? Would you sell it to me? If it's really a *Geochelone gigantea*, I'm willing to give a good price. Where do you live?"

"I have no intention of selling it!" I wrote back with irritation.

"But where do you live? Where did you find it? I told you before — I'm absolutely wild to have that species of tortoise." Something kept me from telling him I lived in Venice. "It doesn't matter where I live," I wrote back. "I have it and that's that. It's not meant to live cooped up in a cage. It's not going to be part of any collection, and I'm not selling it." I switched off the computer without waiting for a response. Then I burst out laughing, imagining the look on his face if I told him that the tortoise he wanted to buy was my grandmother.

Chapter Nine

Little by little, I was getting used to my new grandmother. Without consulting Max, I found other useful information on the Web, such as the best diet for a *Geochelone* in captivity. I bought all different kinds of alfalfa sprouts, along with plenty of apples, oranges, and bananas for the vitamins a tortoise needs. I read that they need a lot of fiber to make their shells and claws hard, and hard-boiled eggs for protein (Nonna swallowed them in the shell, in a single gulp).

I found that she had a passion for red and orange foods. When I offered her a carrot or a slice of watermelon, her little eyes lit up with joy. One day, I discovered her sunk in a puddle of water, about to drop off to sleep. Another day, I came across her wallowing around in the thick mud of a small nearby swamp. When I asked why she got herself all dirty that way, she wrote that it was to keep away the mosquitoes, which were a great nuisance in that season.

Nonna Eia's behavior was changing very rapidly — to put it mildly. Three things still linked her to her human nature:

painting pictures, writing me brief messages in the sand, and performing scenes from Shakespeare (in her own way, that is — pretty emphatically) to give me my cues.

One day, she surprised me, though. In the sand enclosure I found the words, "VALENTINA HAS PAID A VISIT." I was skeptical, but I went to the usual place near the bottomless hull and started digging. I was amazed when out of the earth came a ring with an old *murrina* of Venetian colored glass. The design etched on the glass showed a tiny tree laden with fruit. I recognized it right away — it was Nonna Eia's engagement ring. She'd lost it two years ago while she was working in the garden. And now the red hare had found it and buried it for me. What a momentous gift! I hugged Nonna's long neck and rubbed my face against her wrinkled little tortoise face.

"Aren't you sad that you can't wear it anymore, Nonna?" I asked her. Meanwhile, I put it on the gold chain I wore around my neck, to save for the day when it wouldn't be too big to wear on my finger.

She edged toward the sand enclosure.

"I HAVE NO REGRETS," she wrote. "I'M TOO BUSY FINDING OUT WHAT IT MEANS TO BE HARD OUTSIDE AND SOFT INSIDE."

"So, what does it mean, Nonna?"

"IT MEANS IF YOU'RE HARD OUTSIDE, YOU CAN BE AS SOFT AS YOU LIKE INSIDE," came the cryptic reply.

Since I had no more questions, Nonna rubbed out the writing with her paw and added, "I'M VERY HAPPY, ELISA. AND YET I FEEL HOMESICK."

"You must be lonesome!" I exclaimed in a low voice. I realized what the dark, round splotches in her paintings were. They were other creatures of her species.

The tortoise didn't hear me.

The next day we were in the shed, and Nonna had just finished the umpteenth painting of her island. I must say that for a tortoise, she wasn't a bad artist, now that she'd switched to using her beak instead of her paws. Her paintings had more energy, the colors were stronger, the lines sharper. These paintings had character; to my mind, they could have held their own alongside the pictures shown at the Biennale exhibit. I was no art expert, though, and back then I'd only been to the Biennale one time.

"What are you homesick for, Nonna?" I asked, picking up our conversation from the day before.

This time she thought it over before writing. Then her glinting little eyes glanced at the painting she'd just finished.

"I'M HOMESICK FOR ALDABRA," she wrote in big fat letters.

"You've never even seen Aldabra. I bet you don't even know where it is."

"WHERE IS IT? DO YOU KNOW?"

"It's in the Indian Ocean," I replied. "How can you be homesick for a place you've never been?"

"THAT'S JUST THE WAY IT IS," was her simple answer, accompanied by one of her deep oceanic blasts.

"There's nothing on Aldabra," I explained. "Absolutely nothing. I saw it on the Web. It's just an atoll. The only plants that grow there are dry, thorny shrubs and some mangroves. The rest is all rough black rock, with spiky points as sharp as knives. How much fun could it be to live in a place like that?!"

"FOR ME IT WOULD BE LOTS OF FUN!" she wrote with a kind of fervor. "PONDS OF SWEET FRESH WATER, BIG FLESHY LEAVES, LOTS OF FRIENDLY NEIGHBORS."

"How could I come to see you, Nonna? Aldabra is so far from Venice. I'd miss you!"

"WELL, WHAT CAN YOU DO? WHEREVER YOU ARE, YOU'RE ALWAYS MISSING SOMETHING."

That really hurt. It wasn't like Nonna Eia to answer me so coldly. But after she wrote it, the tortoise gave me a wink. So she didn't think there was any real chance of going to Aldabra.

I blew out a puff of air — a pale imitation of her gigantic snorts — to show my indignation. Still, the suspicion that Nonna Eia could do without her granddaughter lodged in me like a tiny splinter just below the skin — painful only when you touch it.

School had started awhile ago, and it was obvious that I'd have to study much harder than I had in elementary school, just to keep up with my classes. There was so much new material in junior high, so many books to read. I had homework every afternoon when I got home, a task not to be taken lightly. Francesca had gone to a different school, and I felt lonely because I hadn't made any new friends yet. I wanted so much to share my secret with someone, but I didn't know who. Every now and then I thought of Max, the man from the newsgroup who had the private zoo. He loved animals, even if it was in a fanatical collector's strange way; he might know something about giant tortoises that I didn't know. If necessary, I could always get in touch with him again, but not for an instant did I think of revealing the truth. As far as Mamma, now more than ever before, I had to protect Nonna Eia from her. What would she do if she discovered exactly what condition Nonna was in? Never mind a straitjacket — she would think that only some drastic and painful treatment would work for such a sorry state: a ghastly series of electric shock treatments, cold showers, isolation . . . Mamma wouldn't care how much pain she inflicted, if only Nonna could return to normal. And Nonna had said that if she were locked up even for a few days she would die!

No, I was alone, totally alone, and I had to carry on that

way. Having a tortoise for a grandmother took up almost all my free time and gave me many responsibilities, but it also had its fun side. I spent hour after hour observing her. Nonna Eia's habits revealed a hidden and bizarre world. I learned a whole lot of things from her: for instance, how she conserved her energies when she moved, or how she could make the leaves fall from a tree by bumping her back a few times against the trunk. Leaves were one of her favorite foods, and she could devour huge quantities of them. She sometimes used her paw to pick up the biggest ones from the ground and bring them to her mouth. She managed to eat them without dropping a single piece.

Also, Nonna was always ready and willing to perform Shakespeare's plays. In fact, she seemed to love them even more since she'd turned into a tortoise. I had the feeling she was clinging to Shakespeare to keep in touch with whatever part of her human nature still lingered inside her. And I served that purpose too, keeping her anchored to her humanity. As the days went by, I gradually grew more afraid that if I didn't stay nearby, in no time at all Nonna would retreat totally inside her shell, holing up in there and becoming a *Geochelone gigantea* pure and simple, surrendering her stake in humanity forever. But at the same time I also sensed, in a vague way, that Nonna's transformation was a driving force that had nothing to do with me; I had no influence over it whatsoever. Events would take their course regardless of what I could or couldn't do. At best, her love for me and her passion for Shakespeare could only slow down that course.

These were dark thoughts. I tried my best not to dwell on them.

Together we acted out scenes from *Othello*, *Macbeth* (I played the queen and she was the king), and *A Midsummer Night's Dream*. She especially liked the masculine roles and wasn't content simply to give me the cues: Now she recited entire speeches. Day by day I came to understand her better as she performed the roles of King Lear or Mercutio. I can't really explain how that worked — it was sort of like listening to Shakespeare again and again in a foreign language and slowly getting used to the sounds.

It was amazing how her stumpy body could adapt to the dramatic quality of Shakespeare's plays. Her neck was particularly expressive, as she lengthened it or withdrew it to show love or disdain. Hesitation, rage, reluctance, passion — there was no feeling she couldn't represent by an oscillating or sinuous or abrupt movement of that serpentine neck. And that wasn't all. She could weep at Ophelia's death in a truly heartbreaking way, with great jellylike tears that congealed like drops of resin around all the sorrows of the world. Of course, the parts she was best suited for were those that required a certain majestic gravity. Her huge, oceanic blasts accentuated the salient points of the drama and gave them a feeling of relentless destiny.

But her best speech was still Hamlet's monologue "To be

or not to be." Here the tortoise took on all the solemnity and vacillating slowness of the unfortunate, self-absorbed hero. We had found a nice round rock, just the right size for Yorick's skull. Nonna Eia held it tight between her thick scaly forepaws and slowly stretched out her small head till it touched the rock. Then the strangest sounds came from her mouth, interspersed with snorts and blasts rich with grief. I could understand her now, word for word. It's true that by that point I knew the speech by heart, but still I'm sure I really understood her. In fact, little by little something odd was happening: My understanding carried over to her everyday language as well, so that when we talked we didn't need to use the sand enclosure as often. All I had to do was ask her to use words from Shakespeare's plays as much as possible. Our conversations took on a rather elevated tone, but it worked all the same.

So life might have gone on in that quite acceptable way if not for the arrival of a new enemy: winter.

As it got colder, Nonna got even slower. She ate less and less, and her movements kept growing more sluggish. I often found her asleep in the shed, her snout still smeared with paint. She had burrowed out a hole in a corner where the earth was soft. She liked to take shelter in there and could remain motionless for hours at a stretch, curled up in her shell, without making a sound. Sometimes she fell asleep in this position and I couldn't wake her up, even if I yelled loudly or knocked hard on her shell. One good way to wake her was by running a small stick, not too sharp, along the white grooves that surrounded the pentagonal design of her plates. Her shell must have been thinner and more sensitive at those points; maybe she was able to feel something like a tickling, because after a while her head and paws would start coming out and stirring.

But some days not even this method worked, and I didn't know what else to do. I'd get bored. Next thing I knew, my dark thoughts would sneak in through the boredom. How long could Shakespeare and I keep her from losing her human qualities altogether? If someday her transition from one species to another was complete, Nonna Eia and I would find ourselves light-years apart. At those moments, I'd leave some food beside her and go off somewhere, just to run away from my anxiety. I'd go walking around Venice looking for more proof of her self-sufficiency to show Mamma.

I bought an almond pastry in a bakery at the other end of town, a cake with white icing decorated with a pink and blue view of the Rialto bridge in sugar and studded with silvery spots made of more sugar.

"I saw this exact same cake yesterday in a bakery window near San Marco!" Mamma exclaimed.

That was the very place where I'd bought it, but I'd removed the wrapping paper with the store's name and any other signs of where it came from.

"Yes, Nonna told me she copied it from a cake she saw in a store window," I shot back.

Mamma looked at me suspiciously. "Could it be that Nonna said she made it but she really . . . ?"

"I was right there when she rolled out the dough," I replied as coolly as possible.

"Strange. When I was a little girl all she would ever do was act. As far as baking, she was a disaster. You'd never find her in the kitchen fussing with cakes."

"Well, obviously Nonna's become a much better baker since she was just your mother. Who knows, it could happen to you too."

This was a really nasty remark. As a matter of fact my mother had no spare time to bake cakes, and it wasn't very nice of me to remind her. But I needed to distract her and that was just the thing. Mamma started protesting that it wasn't her fault; if she didn't have to work ten hours a day at the newsstand, I'd see what great cakes she could make. I just let her carry on, glad that we were off the subject of Nonna Eia. But from that day on I was much more careful and didn't overdo it by showing her anything too fancy.

One afternoon, I found a message from Max on the computer. He asked me what I'd finally decided. Since I was so worried, I wrote back. At least with him I could talk about the tortoise.

"My *Geochelone* doesn't like winter," I wrote. "Do your reptiles prefer the warm weather too?"

"Hi Elisa, I'm glad to hear from you again. I was afraid we'd lost touch. Winter is long for everyone. Luckily, I have my reptiles for company, and I keep their cages very well heated. I advise you to do the same if you care about your *Geochelone*. Put it in a nice warm cage."

"But I don't keep it in a cage!" I answered as soon as I read his message. "How can you keep a creature imprisoned behind bars and pretend to love it? Maybe you don't really love your reptiles, you just collect them. I want my tortoise to be warm, but I also want it to be free!"

The answer that came the next morning was very peculiar. "Elisa, you've got it all wrong! I love my reptiles very much. They guard my sleep and protect me from nightmares. I'm so tired, Elisa. Tired all the time. Keeping these creatures in cages helps me drive away the phantoms that hunt me down. I've got to keep them locked up — they can only help me if they're under my control. You see, Elisa, every night I dream about witches and giant monsters who want to tear me limb from limb. I wake up frantic with terror, shivering and shaking. Even after I'm awake I'm not in my right mind for a long time, and then I remind myself that I'm the one keeping the monsters prisoner, that there are bars and panes of glass between us, until after a while, I'm not choking with panic anymore. I get back my self-control. As you can see, my reptile collection, all caged in, is better than any medication. I'm so grateful to all those reptiles who are willing to stay locked up in order to save me. They're performing a noble function. They're protecting me, and they know it. They know they're indispensable. What do you call that? I call it love."

I was pretty upset after I read this confession. It made me sort of sick to my stomach. But thinking it over, I decided I could only pity this grown man who was tormented by nightmares like a little baby. Still, I put off answering him.

Weeks went by and the weather got colder; it was the dead of winter in Venice now, with the usual rain, wind, and ice. There was no snow in town, but when I got to Celestia I found the fields covered with little white crystals of frost. The climbing vines on the front of Nonna's house were all withered except for the ivy above the drainpipe. The house itself looked abandoned: The tortoise always slept inside the shed, to avoid having to drag itself up the three steps at the entrance. I was the only human being who went inside, when I needed to cook something or to warm up.

I was really worried. How could a creature from a species used to the tropical sun ever brave the winter? And yet I couldn't face the awful prospect of locking her up in some sort of cage just for warmth. So I kept postponing any decision.

Then one day it happened. The flu and a high fever had kept me away for close to a week, and when I was well enough to go back to Celestia I found Nonna asleep in her hole. I wanted to wake her. I hadn't seen her for so many days, I didn't even know how long she'd been sleeping or how long since she'd had anything to eat.

I tried everything: I tapped, I tugged, I thumped. I used the little stick, pushing the tip hard all along the grooves. Nothing. I decided to try massaging her with almond oil — I remembered that back when she was a woman, she used to like rubbing that into her skin.

I massaged not just the plates of her shell but her head and shoulders too, at least as much as I could reach through the shell's opening. No response. I kept it up, rubbing harder, but it was no use. There was no sign of life in that prehistoric body, except now and then a barely perceptible puff of breath, a far cry from her resounding oceanic snorts. There was nothing more I could do: If I used any more force I might do serious harm.

I could only accept it as a fait accompli: Nonna Eia was in hibernation. And maybe in that hibernation where neither Shakespeare nor I could reach her, she would continue on her slow, mysterious path, down, down, down, further and further away, until she crossed the final border into the blank, indecipherable world of tortoises that awaited her.

Chapter Ten

It wasn't long before I realized there was an even graver threat than the intense cold. Something that could strike suddenly, at any moment.

Flooding.

If only my grandmother had had the good sense to transform into a sea turtle, this wouldn't have posed any danger. I was mad at her for these bizarre choices — they just created more worries for me.

Whenever Venice's waters rose, the shed floor would get flooded, sometimes with more than three feet of water. Saving the paintings had never been a problem: I would simply stack the crates in piles and put the paintings on top until the water flowed out. But this time? What would I do if it happened? I had no idea what might become of a *Geochelone gigantea* if its head went underwater while it was hibernating. Would it drown in its sleep? Besides, for all I knew, her lungs might still retain something of their original human structure. In that case she would die for sure.

What could I do to prevent it? To drag the tortoise from the shed in its deep sleep was out of the question: On my own, I couldn't make it budge a single inch.

My grandmother had been asleep in the cold without touching food or water for more than three weeks now. So I came to a decision.

In my room with the door shut, I went to the animal-lovers' newsgroup and left an SOS message for Max.

"Max, how can I wake my *Geochelone gigantea* from a month-long hibernation without harming it?"

I had to wait till the next day for Max's answer.

"Why do you want to wake it, Elisa?"

"Because it's too cold, and I'm afraid that's no good for it," I answered.

This time Max got back to me right away. "If it's cold where you live, that's why it's hibernating. I told you, you need heat to wake it up. Only heat can do that. You should have a special cage, like the ones I use for my reptiles. The floor is heated by resistance coils. I can get one for you."

"But I don't want to put it in a cage! It couldn't stand that!"

"Tell me, what's the temperature where you live?"

"Very low," I typed. "It's below freezing already."

A few minutes later I had his answer. "That's not a healthy climate for an animal so unsuited to low temperatures. Trust me, Elisa, at least for the winter. I'm sure it would do just fine in one of my cages. In fact, why don't you sell it to me? You could use the money to buy yourself some sweet furry animal."

"I'll never sell it!" I typed. I was fed up with this discussion that was going nowhere.

Max was still at his computer. He wasn't about to give up. "Elisa, I'm really dying to have that kind of tortoise. I'll give you a very good deal on it. What can you do with an animal that's so unsociable? I can help you find something really nice, like a white fox cub, or even an emperor penguin, if you want something unusual. But I'm really set on a *Geochelone*. With that prehistoric majestic look, it would help drive away my monsters better than any other reptile. And I would take extra good care of it. Won't you let me see it at least, Elisa? Then we can talk about it. If you can't part from it, I'll come to wherever you are and help you. I assure you that with my experience I can find a way to wake it from hibernation."

Again I was sure I shouldn't tell him where I lived. This freaky guy with his sick notions was really getting to me. How could I trust someone who kept animals in cages to help him escape from his nightmares? Besides, he was too insistent. I couldn't run that kind of risk. So after a good deal of thought, I typed in this question: "Look, Max, all I want is some information. Could a land tortoise drown if its head is underwater while it's in hibernation?"

Max was still at his computer. He answered right away.

"What a strange question. But have no fear — that couldn't happen because tortoises don't choose holes full of water to hibernate in. Besides, they can keep their heads underwater for up to an hour. You're not telling me that yours has its head underwater, are you?"

"No, its head isn't underwater. But supposing the high water comes while it's asleep? And what if it lasts for more than an hour? What would happen then?" I wrote.

As soon as I sent that anxious message I realized I'd made a mistake. Only we Venetians refer to flooding as "high water" — it was thoughtless of me to mention it. Max could guess where I lived.

And indeed he promptly wrote back. "Why are you talking about high water? Do you by any chance live in Venice?"

"No, I was just supposing," I hurriedly typed. Even to me that answer didn't sound convincing. Worse, it sounded suspicious. I deleted it and shut down the computer.

The Christmas holidays were coming, the temperature had gone up a few degrees, but Nonna still showed no signs of coming out of hibernation.

I was living in a state of high anxiety. At the least sign of possible flooding I would dash to Celestia, even though being near Nonna but unable to move her from the spot was totally pointless.

I would sit beside her, stroking her back and running the

tip of the stick along the hollows between her plates. I would listen to her very faint breathing, the only reassuring sign that she was still alive. I missed our talks. I tried reciting some Shakespearean monologues but she didn't respond. What could be happening inside that fast-asleep little head?

I sat with my back leaning up against her shell and let my mind wander, thinking about myself and my future. If Nonna had been transformed this way, could the same thing happen to me when I was an old woman? What about my mother? Deep down, I didn't think anything like that could happen to Mamma. She was too practical, too down-to-earth, she didn't while away the time reciting Shakespeare, she didn't play Blindman's Buff along the winding alleys of Venice. No, there was no danger of Mamma turning into any kind of odd creature.

But what about me? Nonna Eia and I were as alike as two drops of water; even my name was close to hers. Would I go crazy someday too? Would I be locked up in a madhouse? Or could I transform myself all at once, at the first try, into . . . into what? Nonna had never told me what those women in her stories changed into, the women from that ancient race at the far ends of the earth who refused to die. I'd have to ask her as soon as she woke up.

As soon as she woke up . . . but when she came out of hibernation, would she still be able to answer me?

I forced my mind away from all that and went back to thinking about myself.

The idea of becoming a *Geochelone gigantea* didn't appeal to me. I was thinking more of . . . I don't know, a bird or a fawn maybe. I didn't know if you could choose, but probably you could. Nonna had gotten her inspiration from the tortoise-shell comb, so maybe I could find mine in a bird's feather. A seagull's feather. Did I want to be a seagull? Why not? Or from a deer's antler. That wouldn't be bad, becoming a deer. They run so beautifully! Or I could become an elephant, because they live very long too, and that's certainly something to consider when you're choosing a new identity. A lovely gray lady elephant. But anyhow, I didn't want to become a reptile like Nonna when I was old, that was for sure.

I shook off my fantasies with an urge to start running, to escape. After all, it was a long way off! I was still only ten. That was far from Nonna's eighty years. I still had my whole life to live!

I turned around for a peep at Nonna Eia. She was as motionless as a boulder, gray and silent. Was she dreaming? What would tortoises in hibernation dream about? Some orange food? Maybe she was dreaming about Shakespeare. Or Aldabra? Or all three together, like in those incoherent dreams I'd been having lately, dreams where you can't make sense of anything.

Sitting there beside her for hours, I brooded about our future. To my great surprise, I found myself thinking quite often of what would be the right thing to do if, once she woke from hibernation, the tortoise had completely lost interest in human concerns. Much as I hated the idea of parting from her, if I were really a loving granddaughter I would find some way to take her to Aldabra. That was where she belonged. She would feel safe there, on the island where her species had flourished for thousands of years.

Come to think of it, however far it was, Aldabra wasn't on the moon, after all. It was a real place, at a real geographical location on this planet. I could send her on a ship heading down there. I just had to find a way. It was important for her. On that remote island she'd fit right in with the other creatures of her species; she could make a new life. Here in Venice she had no one but me. And what if I got sick again? How long could this drag on? Not that I was exactly tired of it . . . but how long could I hold out?

Lots of times I'd start to cry, worn out by all the silence, until one day, to make myself think about something else, I decided to focus on the practical side of my crazy plan. Just to see if it could be done.

For a start, I had to get back in touch with Max. I didn't see any other solution. Who else could I talk to about the *Geochelone*?

When I sat down at the computer I was firm and concise.

"Max, I want to take my tortoise to Aldabra. How can I do it?"

"Are you kidding?" Max wrote back a few hours later. "I'm telling you, let me have it. I'll take very good care of it. It'll be the queen of my reptile collection."

"No, I've told you a thousand times, I don't want it to be in a cage. If you won't help me, I'll go to some international organization for wildlife preservation."

Actually, nothing of the sort had occurred to me until that very moment. I knew Aldabra was a wildlife sanctuary, a refuge that was regarded as part of the universal heritage, where these tortoises, in danger of extinction, were protected. But I was afraid of what the scientists might ask. What could I say if they wanted to know where I got my *Geochelone*? Still, they would help me get it to Aldabra. Maybe. Or maybe they would lock it up in a cage too. . . .

The screen was flashing that I had mail.

"Elisa, don't do anything till I get there. I promise I'll help you. Tell me where you live."

I hesitated for a split second, then shut down the computer.

Chapter Eleven

The last day of school before Christmas vacation, and was I relieved! I'd have more time to devote to Nonna and wouldn't have to leave her alone for so many hours at a stretch. Even though sitting next to her while she slept wasn't all that much fun. I had to find a way to wake her up.

I was working out a new scheme for getting through the winter. I'd decided to build a hothouse inside the shed, around Nonna, though I didn't know yet exactly how. Not a cage with bars, but a transparent hothouse, warm and comfortable, so when she woke up she wouldn't feel she was in a prison.

I sat in class pondering how I'd build this glass structure, only dimly aware of what was going on around me. At their desks, my rowdy classmates couldn't wait to be released. Their shrieks and calls and bursts of laughter went right past me. Everyone was listening for the sound of the bell, to shoot out of the classroom and fling themselves into the long vacation, like fish out of water, gasping for their ponds.

Anyhow, what I could do was put up glass walls all around

her and light a wood fire inside. That way, the air would warm up and Nonna would come out of hibernation. Afterward, I could take her to some safe place.

It was a stroke of genius, only I wasn't sure how to make it a reality. First of all, I needed some panes of glass, some boards, and putty to hold it all together. I might be able to get the glass from the windows of her house, or better still, buy it, if it wasn't too expensive. I could make the hothouse in the shape of a pyramid — that way it would be better balanced.

"What's with you, Elisa? Aren't you going home?"

I gave a start. The sound of the bell was echoing in my ears. I looked around and realized I was all alone in the classroom.

"What do you kids think about all day long?" The teacher, standing very straight at the door, was regarding me with a kind of indulgent surprise.

I got up from my seat. "I was thinking . . . about what to give my grandmother for Christmas." It wasn't a lie: The hothouse would be my Christmas present to Nonna Eia.

I left school and rushed to get to the stores before they closed. I wanted to find out right away how much the panes of glass cost, but I didn't know where they were sold. So I wandered around looking in store windows till I found one displaying ceramic tiles. Maybe they sold glass as well. I went in to find out.

They only sold bathroom fixtures, but they told me where

I could find panes of glass. It was far from my house, so I decided to go the next afternoon. It was late already, and Mamma was expecting me for dinner.

As I entered I heard a man's voice coming from the living room. It sounded young. Who could it be? We didn't have visitors very often in our aquarium-like apartment. Maybe it was the man who read the gas meter, or the plumber for some repair, so I went into the bathroom to wash my hands.

"Elisa, is that you? Come here right away! This minute!"

What did I do? I couldn't recall breaking anything recently, or clogging up the bathroom sink with my hair again. It couldn't be any ancient toy that fell on someone's head either, because I hadn't thrown anything off the balcony, at least I didn't think so. But Mamma's tone was unmistakable: I'd definitely done something.

I went into the living room.

What I saw left me speechless. A young guy in a threadbare suede jacket was sitting in the armchair. He wasn't a plumber; he wasn't wearing any sort of overalls. He seemed like a cartoon teenager, with his prominent Adam's apple bobbing up and down, his hunched shoulders, and his knees pressed tight together with his feet turned inward. I thought he looked like someone who was desperate to pee. He had light-blue watery eyes ringed by dark circles, which made him look as if he'd been up all night. His hair was reddish-blond, and his complexion was wan. He was painfully thin — his arms and legs seemed almost shrunken. He looked as though he were being *forced* to sit there, on the verge of leaping up and darting away. And yet he greeted me with a good-natured smile.

Mamma was standing near the window with her arms folded and a cigarette between her lips; she stared at me with a curious, stern expression, in contrast to our unknown visitor's bright look that masked his embarrassment.

"What's this story about a giant tortoise?" she asked brusquely, putting out her cigarette in one quick, furious motion. "Where is this tortoise anyway?"

I looked from my mother to the Adam's apple of the man in the chair. He kept smiling at me, a broad, expectant smile.

"What tortoise?" I stammered. But of course I'd caught on.

"I'm Max," said the man, starting to get up. Then, as if reconsidering — maybe I seemed too young for such a formal greeting — he sank back down in his chair. "Hi, Elisa. Nice to meet you in person."

I was trapped! I looked at the guy, I looked at Mamma, seeking some plausible way out. Nothing came to me except to deny everything.

"This young man has been telling me that you found him online. Is that true?"

"Yes," I murmured. There seemed no point in denying that.

"And you told him you have an enormous tortoise from some strange island. . . . I can't remember the name."

"Aldabra," the man said, crossing his legs. I could see he was doing everything possible to appear at ease.

"Aldabra," Mamma repeated, lowering her head. She started to light a new cigarette then changed her mind and once more folded her arms over her chest. "I'd like very much to hear your explanation of this story, Elisa. If it's not too much trouble, that is, seeing that you're not in the habit of telling me anything you do."

"I was bored one day, so I made up a story about having a giant tortoise," I confessed, shrugging my shoulders. "This man took me seriously, and it was fun to continue the joke. That's the whole story."

"And you gave him your address." Mamma's voice tensed up. This, for her, was the crux of the matter.

"No, I didn't give it to him!" I blurted. "Actually, excuse me, Mister, uh, Max, but how did you find me? How did you know where I live? I never told you!" To make my accusation stronger, I addressed him very formally, not at all in the casual tone of our e-mails.

Mamma wheeled around to face him. The man cleared his throat. His Adam's apple jiggled. "I'm a computer whiz. I know how to do searches of addresses from newsgroups. . . .

It's not that hard. And you did mention high water, Elisa. From that it didn't take much to figure out you must live in Venice. The hard part came later. Let's just say I made some careful inquiries."

"And just why did you make those inquiries, Mister . . . Max?" my mother asked in a very controlled tone. I could practically see the anger surging up inside her. "What exactly brought you here?"

"I fully intend to purchase the *Geochelone gigantea* that your daughter claims to own!" he exclaimed emphatically, all his awkwardness vanishing for the moment. "I'm ready to give her a good price. But I'd have to see the tortoise first."

Mamma looked at me again, her eyes like two question marks.

"I don't have any tortoise," I cried. "I told you, I made it all up! I was just kidding around. That's not a crime, is it?"

"But why would you do that, Elisa?" Mamma asked, baffled. My little quirks always got her flustered. They made her feel insecure.

"Just for fun."

She seemed almost disappointed that there wasn't any tortoise. She unfolded her arms, which had been pressed tight against her chest, and spread them out in a resigned gesture, as if to say she couldn't make any sense of all this.

"But . . . but . . . I'm positive this child has a *Geochelone gigan-*

tea hidden somewhere!" The young man rose from his chair and pointed a finger at me. Standing at his full height, he was extremely tall. His whole wispy body trembled with indignation. "I'm sure of it! Absolutely sure!" he kept repeating as we stared at him, flabbergasted. "It wasn't any joke. You . . . you knew all sorts of things about that kind of tortoise. Things you couldn't find in any scientific journal! The way it snorts — you described it exactly right. Where could you have learned that if you don't have a real, live tortoise?" His bulging eyes glittered, moving from one to the other of us, imploring. He's about to burst into tears, I thought, watching him wag his finger. He was totally losing it!

Mamma frowned. Hearing him speak so vehemently, she was starting to waver again, I could tell. "My daughter can be a bit eccentric sometimes. You mustn't let it get to you. . . . But look, think it over. How could my Elisa hide such a huge tortoise?" she asked in a faint voice. She seemed to be asking herself the same thing.

"I don't know, I don't know! But I assure you, from the details she gave me . . . She said that when the weather turned cold it went into hibernation, which means it couldn't be in here. Your apartment is nice and warm. Do you have a garden? Or some . . . some open space?"

Mamma turned swiftly to me, a questioning look on her face. The word "garden" jogged her memory.

"Elisa, this joke wouldn't by any chance have something to do with Nonna Eia?"

To get out of this one I'd have to come up with some diversion right away.

I looked down. "No, it's nothing to do with her. I'll tell what happened, Mister Max," I murmured slowly, as if I were very reluctant. "You kept urging me to . . . to meet you in the Biennale Gardens after school. . . . You said you had a nice present for me. . . . So I decided to have some fun and tease you a bit by making up a story about a giant tortoise. I didn't say so before because Mamma doesn't want me talking to strangers, even on the Web."

"Get out! Out of my house! I'm warning you, I'll call the police! Elisa, go to your room! I'll deal with you later!"

In a rage, Mamma seized the telephone like a madwoman.

The man took a step toward me, his arm outstretched, his trembling finger pointed as if he wanted to stab me through the heart. "That's all a lie! You're a liar!" he snarled.

"Get out of here!" Mamma screamed. "Leave my child alone!" Meanwhile her finger was frantically pressing the phone buttons.

Max wheeled around to face her. What he saw must have scared him because he quickly lowered his arm and started retreating toward the door. He kept walking backward, tripping several times on the rug. He was even paler than before, but the weird thing was that instead of looking furious, he looked guilty. He opened his mouth as if to protest, then changed his mind. He turned his back on us and without a word made it to the door, flung it open, and raced down the stairs.

Mamma let the phone drop — she was shaking much too hard to finish dialing — and slammed the door shut. I took advantage of that moment to slink off to my room.

I curled up on my bed waiting for the storm to burst. Better that than questions about the tortoise. I was sure that had completely slipped her mind by this point. Her child pursued by a maniac! That was a much more serious matter than having a daughter who made up stories about giant tortoises, in league with her grandmother. Still, it bothered me a lot that I had accused an innocent person. Mamma might think it over and actually carry out her threat to call the police. Some other mother, more sure of herself, would have done it on the spot. I didn't even want to think about that. I told myself this was my first and only time: Never again would I blame a person for something he hadn't done.

What I wasn't prepared for was tears. My mother came into my room with glistening eyes. I could see she'd really had a scare. She was scared for me. She was angry too, that was only natural, but what she said made my heart melt.

"Elisa, what were you thinking?" she murmured, sitting down beside me on the bed. "That man could have hurt you, don't you understand? Really hurt you."

I hugged her tight. "No, Mamma," I said on impulse. "I made it all up. He never asked me to meet him in the Gardens."

She stared at me, mystified. "Then why did you say so?"

"I wanted him to go away. I didn't like him."

At that, the storm burst. Mamma's words were hard, freezing hailstones that crashed into me with fury. She accused me of all kinds of wickedness, she gave me a glimpse of hellfire, until she wore herself out and simmered down. Her voice turned soft, almost meek.

"I think I haven't been spending enough time with you," she murmured, her hands automatically hunting for the cigarette that wasn't there. "If only your father were here. . . . I just can't do it all on my own. . . . If he were still alive, he would know what to do."

My heart flipped over. This was awful!

We were silent for a moment, then she pulled herself together, as if the full impact of what I'd done suddenly struck her all over again. "I can't trust you anymore!" she yelled. "You lied! You accused an innocent man! You invented a tortoise that doesn't exist! Why? Why? Why? You're so peculiar, so strange, just like . . . What am I going to do with you?"

Strange like . . . who? Like Nonna Eia? I said nothing, just looked down at the floor waiting for the wave of anger to pass. It was agony, seeing her so upset, but what else could I say without giving away my secret?

"I love you," I finally managed to whisper. "You're a wonderful mom, I really mean it. The best mom in the world."

"It's not easy, trying to figure you out," she moaned. "But I love you too. You're all I have."

I breathed a sigh of relief. Now that we could cuddle up and feel close, I realized how much I needed this.

I stretched out so I could rest my head in her lap, then took her hand and brought it to my cheek. I felt a surge of love for her. From now on, I thought, things are going to be fine between us.

Just then the siren blared.

"It's the flood warning," I whispered in dismay.

"I'd better go stack up the newspapers at the kiosk," Mamma sighed, as if she too hated to part from me. She pinched me lightly on the cheek. "I heard on the radio today that the water level is going to break every record from the past ten years."

Chapter Twelve

High water! And Nonna Eia totally comatose. I was so frantic that I thought even imminent death couldn't shock her out of hibernation.

My mom was taken by surprise when I suddenly leaped from the bed, and she reached out to pull me back. "Where are you going?"

I was at the door before she could catch up.

"There's something I've got to do!"

"All of a sudden? What is it?"

"It's too long to go into!"

"Don't forget your coat, it's cold out!" she shouted after me.

I was already on the street, wearing a jacket I grabbed from a hook beside the door.

I raced along, jostling any passersby who got in my way in the narrow alleys, exchanging pushes and shoves. My heart was pounding a mile a minute, driven by the mournful whine of the siren that spread throughout Venice. It reminded me of war movies. But my fellow Venetians were all calm and methodical as they swiftly rolled up the shutters of their stores — a routine they'd gone through thousands of times. Some people were already setting up wooden gangplanks at strategic points.

In Venice, high water is something you learn to accept patiently and take in stride. In the stores, the merchandise has to be placed on high shelves so it doesn't get wet. The rugs are rolled up. As if by magic, all the people on the street are suddenly wearing knee-high rubber boots. From one minute to the next, a party mood springs up. No one gives in to fear of flooding.

The only one in the entire city who was scared was me. I kept on running with my hand pressed to my side, where I was starting to feel stabs of pain.

In ten minutes I was in Celestia.

Crossing the footbridge, I quickly checked the water level in the lagoon. The rubble-strewn beach was already completely underwater. I ran steadily on, driven forward, heedless of anyone who crossed my path.

The *Casermette*.

I ran past the houses, paying no attention to the people busily taking in whatever was scattered in the gardens. No one stopped me. No one asked where I was dashing off to in such a hurry.

The sirens had stopped. How much time did I have? An hour? Two? I had no idea what I would do once I got there. I'd worry about that later. Right now I just had to keep moving.

I got to the neglected gardens and the shipyard arch, then ran along the path up to the gate with the MILITARY ZONE sign. I passed the signs saying DANGER OF COLLAPSE and threaded my way through the brambles. By the time I reached Nonna Eia's shed, the blood in my head was pounding furiously. I stopped to take a deep breath, then another. After I filled up my lungs for the third time, I raced inside.

Nonna Eia hadn't stirred from the little hole where she lay smooth and motionless as a big gray boulder. The hole was in a shallow dip in the floor of the shed: It was the first place that would fill up with water.

Still panting, I stared fixedly at the protruding hump of the big shell. The tortoise was virtually stuck inside the dug-out hollow. She was so huge. How could I ever get her out? I looked around frantically.

I needed to warm up the air around her, I thought, still panting with my mouth open to catch my breath. I'd have to build some kind of makeshift hothouse around her with whatever materials I could find, so she'd wake up and get herself out of that wretched hole.

Not a single window was left in the shed, but there were still some in good condition in her old house.

As I raced toward Nonna's cottage, I realized I had no idea how to get the panes of glass out of their frames. Then, in the cluttered hallway piled with ponchos and umbrellas, it dawned on me that I could make use of what was right there, staring me in the face.

I didn't have the time or the skill to build a glass hothouse; I'd have to make do with plastic. Nonna's ponchos were long and wide. They would do the trick. I found three: a yellow, a green, and a red, all different sizes. I'd sew them together to make a tent.

In a drawer of the kitchen table, next to a big pile of beeswax candles, I found a box of toothpicks. I could use them as pins. I took one out and tried puncturing the thin plastic of one of the ponchos. It worked! I lined up the ponchos and pinned them together as best I could. Now I had to find a post to prop them up, and something to give off heat. The candles! I needed wood too, to make a decent fire. And matches to light it.

The matches were near the stove. But I had to search everywhere for the pole to hold it all in place. I finally decided that the longest broomstick would be just the thing.

I carried all this back to the shed and went over to the tortoise.

"Get ready to rise and shine, Nonna," I said, and started working the broomstick into the ground alongside the hole where she lay. I rotated it in the dirt, shoving it in really hard and deep so it wouldn't collapse and bring the whole tent down with it. When it seemed firm and upright, I pushed a heap of dirt around it with my foot to keep it stable. Then I got to work setting up the three colored plastic ponchos around it, making sure that this slapdash tent was enclosing Nonna's hole. I worked on it from the outside, though, to make the job easier. At that point it struck me that I had nothing to fasten the ponchos to the stick, so I dashed back into the house to look for some twine. I found ribbons from old gift wrapping, all neatly rolled up. They would do just as well.

What finally took shape, after about ten minutes of work, was a kind of multicolored Indian wigwam, anchored to the already damp ground by big rocks. I'd arranged it so that the tent opened on one side — that way I could wriggle my way in. If I didn't bump into it too hard, it would stay up.

Now for the wood. I ran outside to look around. I needed dry wood to make a nice, warming fire. But where could I find it? The dead branches on the trees were no good — they were damp from the last few days of rain. I went back in the house, determined to break up some old chairs if I had to. Whirling through the rooms like a tornado, I grabbed every small wooden thing I could lay my hands on.

A rolling pin for pasta dough, the chopping board, a few wooden hangers, a pair of Indian bowls, a handful of clothespins, some picture frames, a jewelry box (I hesitated a second over that because it seemed too valuable, but in the end

I added it to the pile), a statuette of Buddha. Last of all I took a straw hat hanging on a nail.

The things were all old, the wood nicely weathered. I also took some newspapers that were yellowed with age. And with that heap of stuff piled in my arms, I returned to the shed.

I slid inside the tent, careful not to bump into the broomstick so it wouldn't all come crashing down. It was impossible to see inside there, so I lit a match. There was barely space for me to curl up next to the shell resting in its hole. I lit a candle and looked around for somewhere to put it, but no luck. So I decided on Nonna's shell. I dripped a little wax onto the central plate and stuck the candle in it. The tortoise didn't move. I couldn't even tell for sure if I could hear her very faint breathing or was just imagining it.

For starters, I lit all the candles and set them around the first one. That turned Nonna into a kind of giant birthday cake, and the inside of the tent glowed with a soft, flickering light. I crumpled the pages of the newspaper and placed them as far as possible from the tortoise, making sure they didn't touch the tent. I didn't want to set Nonna on fire. I only wanted to wake her up.

Then I put all the wooden things on top of the newspaper, the biggest ones on the bottom, the smallest on top. I had to be careful not to set the plastic on fire either.

All this time, I was so intent on my work that I hadn't even looked around. Only now did I notice that the ground beneath me was all soggy and muddy.

High water!

Time was running out. No decent fire would burn on really wet ground. I lit a match and held it to the newspaper. It caught right away and burned fast. Too fast. Would it last long enough for the wood to catch fire?

I crumpled up another sheet of paper very tight and tossed it on. Then another. Finally the straw hat caught fire and the flames spread to one of the hangers. First the fire died down, but then the flames brightened and sprang back to life. They were so close! I could feel their scorching caress on my face. A picture frame caught fire with a merry crackling. The flames were very high now, practically grazing us. The picture frame was blazing — it was like a miracle. Success!

I looked at Nonna. She still lay motionless, her head and paws out of sight. The heat down there was so intense it felt like the flames of hell. Why didn't she wake up? Big drops of sweat trickled down my forehead. I was so hot! I was about to pass out! The tortoise couldn't help but be hot too! I lifted my hand from the ground — it was wet and smeared with mud. I could feel the water under my legs. At this rate, it would come to a boil any minute. I had to keep brushing away the tiny sparks that hit my knees.

But the tortoise slept on!

The flames began turning blue and sending out loud crackles.

The crackling and sputtering went on for a couple of minutes, then came a smothered, hissing sound. So my fire turned out to be pretty pathetic — already it was going out.

Everything was totally wet and muddy. I bent down to see how much water was in Nonna's hole, but just then the fire fizzled out pitifully, giving off a thick acrid smoke that stayed trapped inside the tent.

I started coughing. My eyes burned and teared so badly that I had to close them.

The smoke was choking me. I couldn't stop coughing. Either I had to get out or else let some air in the tent. I stretched out my hand to open it, groping with my eyes closed. *Air! Air!*

A faint noise stopped me in my tracks.

What was it?

A low, drawn-out sound. Like a bellows. Or . . . an oceanic snort . . .

I made myself open my eyes, and through my tears I could see the tortoise's head just peeking out. Bit by bit, it was thrusting forward. Nothing else happened for a minute or so, and then, amid the thick plumes of smoke, the neck began to stretch. A moment later the whole shell, encircled by the flaming candles, started rising straight up, coming unstuck from the swampy ground with a great plop and lifting itself above the hole.

It must have been the smoke that did it. "Nonna!" I shrieked, hugging and kissing her tiny head. "You're awake!"

I sprang to my feet and in my eagerness banged against the broomstick. The tent gave way, drifting down onto my head and onto the tortoise. The candles went out. I flung my arms around to work my way out of the plastic and the smoke. I squirmed and struggled until I was free, then yanked off the ponchos covering Nonna's back. At last we were away from that acrid smoke.

"Come on, we have to hurry or you'll fall asleep again!" I cried with the last ounce of breath I had left.

The tortoise seemed still in a daze, unaware of any danger. Three burned-out candles stood upright on her back. I knocked them off with my hand — they made her look so silly. She moved her front paws in a strenuous effort to clamber up out of the hole. Then, at her usual slow pace, she started making her way through the muddy water. I sloshed along behind, pushing on her shell with both hands to hurry her toward the door of the shed. The water was halfway up my legs by now.

"Hurry, hurry, don't stop," I shouted. Could she still understand me? Was it still Nonna Eia, this slow, heavy creature who'd been asleep for weeks?

Whoever it was, it moved. At long last we were out of the shed. I kept pushing the tortoise, wondering all the while where I could take it. Inside the house would be best, but I didn't think I could swing it. The last few times Nonna had gone up the three stairs at the entrance, it had taken forever, and now, on top of that, she was half-dazed, not even wide awake. Besides, staying on the ground floor wouldn't do any good. At high water that could be flooded. Only the second floor was safe, but that, unfortunately, was out of the question.

So I gave up the idea of the house and pushed the tortoise toward the highest part of the meadow. This was a mound, a low hill around six or eight feet high with bright green grass. Even the frost never reached that far up. I didn't know if the water had ever gotten up there in the past, but I didn't think so. For the moment, anyway, I had no better solution. So I urged Nonna on, shoving and tugging, splashing through the meadow that had become a swamp, until I got her all the way to the top of the hill. The last stretch, which was very steep, I couldn't accomplish without her cooperation. Luckily, the tortoise was a bit more wide awake and seemed to grasp what I was trying to do.

Up at the top we were finally on dry land. I threw myself down on the cool grass; it was hardly even damp. I was totally wiped out. "Nonna, don't go back to sleep. Say something to me, please!"

The tortoise turned her little reptilian head toward me, and

I thought I saw her smile. She let out a snort, followed by some of her strange noises. It sounded to me like, "Thank you, Elisa, you saved my life."

My heart swelled with joy, and I let out a sigh of relief, but at that exact moment I heard a noise coming from the house. I looked up and caught sight of something moving behind the open front door. Someone was spying on us from inside!

I stood up to get a better look.

I was sure I saw a shadow appear, then disappear.

"Who's there?" I called.

Beside me, Nonna Eia puffed and stretched out her neck.

The shadow emerged from the shelter of the doorway and came toward us, kicking up splashes with each step. It was wearing high rubber boots. The water — knee-high, just below the rim of the boots — slowed it down.

"Mamma . . ." I stammered. I stood there stunned, watching her moving toward us like someone on stilts. She had to raise her legs high with each step to struggle her way through the water, which had overrun the meadow below our hill. As she approached, the expression on her face was so dumbfounded, such a picture of shock and astonishment, that I burst out in wild laughter.

Chapter Thirteen

She came to a halt three feet away from us. Her eyes were aghast and stayed glued on me, deliberately avoiding the sight of the gigantic tortoise at my side.

"I can't find Nonna Eia," she said in a wisp of a voice. "She's not in the house."

I stopped laughing. "What on earth are you doing here?" I asked. Only just then did I realize how unusual it was for her to come looking for Nonna, disobeying her orders.

I didn't really expect an answer. I expected her to throw a fit and bombard me with questions about my unusual companion. She was obviously unhinged by what she saw. And yet she stubbornly ignored it, as if the tortoise were invisible.

"You ran out like a lunatic. I couldn't follow you right away — I had to stack up the newspapers so they wouldn't get wet, and that's something that can't wait. But when you raced away I was sure you were dashing over here to Nonna Eia's. So as soon as I finished with the papers I decided to come after you. I went in the house but I didn't find her. Elisa, you have to believe me, I . . . I miss my mother so much. I know she doesn't want to see me, but just for a minute . . . I'd just wish her Merry Christmas and then leave. Where is she? Tell the truth: Did she hide when she saw me coming?"

I tried to think. Certain things had to be dealt with immediately while others could wait. This wasn't the right moment to explain to Mamma that Nonna Eia had been transformed into the tortoise beside me. I stood there gaping, an idiotic little smile pasted to my lips. I was beginning to suspect that the tortoise really was invisible to everyone except me.

Nonna Eia stirred and let out one of her loud blasts. Finally, very reluctantly, my mother shifted her eyes from me to glance over in that direction.

"It's enormous! Gigantic! Elisa, why did you lie to me? You swore over and over that you made it up. Why?"

I didn't answer.

"We'll discuss this at home. . . ." she began in a harsh tone. But she broke off abruptly, as if struck by something. As she gazed, frowning, at the tortoise crouched on the ground, something new crept into her face, a kind of awesome wonder.

"There's something familiar about it. . . . I have the feeling I've seen it before," Mamma said. "It's looking at me as if . . . Where did you find it?"

Nonna Eia's small eyes were fixed on Mamma. They had an unusual sparkle, very alive, very human. There was a moment of mute suspense, then she lifted her left front paw from the ground and with slow gravity, raised it up. At the same time, she leaned her long neck to the left and brought her paw gently to the top of her head. Nonna Eia stayed that way for a long moment, her paw on her head, her eyes trained on the woman who was staring at her as if to say: Oh, good grief!

My mom seemed in a trance as she stepped forward toward the tortoise. When she was very close, she crouched down till her own head was level with that odd little head.

Just then the tortoise's jaws opened in a great yawn. She shut her mouth. Then yawned again.

"Oh, my God!" The words escaped from my mother. "Oh, my God! Oh no! That fragrance . . . It's . . . It's . . ." I understood that a whiff of jasmine and spices must have hit her full in the face. I understood something else too. Those sudden yawns were a clear warning. I had witnessed them often enough before: Nonna was literally famished. Well, no wonder! She hadn't eaten in weeks.

I gazed around, trying to figure out what I could give her. There must be some cabbages left in the garden. I couldn't keep her waiting another minute.

"I'm going to find her something to eat, Mamma. I'll be right back."

I doubt if Mamma even heard me, but the *Geochelone* gave a vigorous nod of approval. Big tears glittered in her dark eyes.

I ran down the hill in search of cabbages and carrots, splashing in water up to my calves. In my haste I was pulling up half-drowned carrots with gobs of muddy soil clinging to the roots. The cabbages were turning yellow and the carrots were rotting, but I couldn't waste time hunting for anything better.

Two minutes later, I was back.

Mamma and Nonna hadn't moved, but something had changed. They seemed to be closer, and really communicating. Mamma's hands trembled as they lightly touched the chilly skin. I set the food down on the ground but they didn't even notice.

They were moaning and muttering. Both of them. Then Mamma began blurting all sorts of incoherent words and broken phrases. I tried hard to make sense of them. All at once they began to fit together — a torrent of rapid exclamations.

"It's you! It's you! That gesture, your hand on top of your head . . . You did that all the time when I was a little girl, whenever I made you laugh! I used to say, 'Mamma, why are you putting your hand on your head?' And you always said the same thing, 'It's so my happiness can't fly away. It'll escape unless you keep it inside.' Oh . . . Mamma! And your perfume, 'Wild Breeze.' Well, you're certainly wild now. . . . You finally got what you wanted, didn't you?" She laughed and talked nonsense, stroking and embracing her all the time, bending down to brush her lips on the top of Nonna's head.

I couldn't believe my eyes. What was going on? Were all my fears way off base? And they recognized each other right away? In all of three minutes? So the saying is really true — blood is thicker than water.

It was as if the blood stirring up inside Mamma had taught her all she needed to know about life. Something within her had broken through its barriers; part of her secret self was erupting and flowing out like a stream of lava. She was freed from the lifelong fears that had forced her to reject so fiercely everything the least bit strange and mysterious.

And the tortoise's passionate murmurings revealed her complete forgiveness for all that had gone before.

"LET'S HAVE A LOOK AT YOU. YOU'VE HARDLY CHANGED IN ALL THESE YEARS," she was mumbling, with puffs and contented marine snorts.

"What? What is she telling me?" Mamma couldn't understand. How could she? It had taken me quite some time, and I only succeeded in the end thanks to Shakespeare.

"She said you haven't changed a bit," I explained.

"Well, I can't say the same of you!" my mother declared, laughing and crying at the same time.

"Do you know how long a *Geochelone gigantea* lives?" I said, turning to Mamma. "A hundred and fifty years or more. So Nonna Eia won't have to die for a long time, right, Nonna?"

The tortoise nodded, slowly and ponderously.

"Yes, but . . . what kind of life will she have?"

"A tortoise's life!"

"Why didn't you ever say anything about it? Why?"

I shrugged my shoulders. She knew quite well why I never said anything.

"How long has she been . . . in this condition?"

While Nonna started gobbling up the cabbages, I told my mother about the slow, imperceptible transformation that had taken place, and how happy it had made Nonna Eia.

"Aren't these animals cold in winter? I don't think Venice is a healthy place for her. . . . It's so damp!"

"Yes, that's a problem," I agreed, watching Nonna eagerly finish off the carrots. "She's constantly slipping into hibernation."

"She needs to be taken somewhere . . . somewhere suitable."

"Not a zoo!" I exclaimed in fright. "And not an institution, Mamma!"

"No, no, what are you thinking . . . ?"

Nonna Eia let out a raging snort. Mamma turned to her. "No, no, I wasn't even thinking of that!"

"And no nursing home either," I added emphatically.

"I was thinking . . . now that we're together again, I don't want to lose her. We could bring her home. The attic is big and has that roof terrace. We can turn up the heat and keep her nice and cozy. She'll live with us forever. Right, Mamma? Don't you want to live with us?"

Nonna hesitated, her head swaying from side to side, then gave out a bellow. She was saying yes.

"We've got to take her home right away! How, though? What will people say if we go through the streets?"

The tortoise made some noises but I couldn't understand. She snorted, then tried again, more clearly.

"By boat. She's telling us to bring her home in a boat," I translated. "We've got to get going, Mamma. It's cold and she could slip back into hibernation."

"Right, a boat . . . Where can we find one?"

"I'll go look," I suggested. "I know of someone here in Celestia who has a big motorboat."

"I'd better go too. He might not be willing to rent it to you."

"And leave Nonna here alone?" I looked doubtfully at the tortoise.

"DON'T WORRY, ELISA. I WON'T FALL ASLEEP," Nonna said, her head swaying.

"What? What's she saying? Why can you understand her and I can't?" Mamma was impatient. She automatically searched for her cigarettes but didn't find them. "We'll be back as fast as we can," she promised after I translated, and she hugged the thin reptilian neck and stroked her head. Tears glistened in her eyes, and she had a shy smile I'd never seen before.

After some last-minute warnings not to fall asleep, we left

Nonna and headed down to the meadow. We were surprised to note that while the three of us had been up on the hill, the water below had completely receded. We hurried on, turning around every few minutes to check the hill. High up on top, the tortoise was silhouetted against the red twilight sky.

We reached the *Casermette* as fast as we could, and I pointed out the house of the man with the motorboat. We knocked. His wife opened the door and looked us over with some surprise, as Mamma explained that we needed the boat just for an hour: We had to bring something home from Celestia, a heavy piece of furniture, an old chest of drawers.

I stood in shocked silence, marveling at her: It was the first time I'd ever heard her make up a story.

The woman didn't ask questions. She said her husband had gone out but left the motorboat moored nearby, and she was willing to accept the payment Mamma offered. Everything was going fantastically.

We brought the boat as close as possible to the path that led to Nonna's house and docked it at the shore. With a little luck we could manage to bring the tortoise down there without anyone seeing us. Then, once we got on the boat, we'd throw something over her to cover her. We'd get to the canal right below our house. And with a little more luck we'd cross the final stretch to our door without being seen. After that, all we had to do was bring back the motorboat, and we were home free.

But when we looked up at the mound in the middle of the meadow, there was no bulging shape breaking the clear, gently rounded outline of the hill. Was it the light playing tricks on us? The sky was growing darker.

We hurriedly climbed up the slope only to confirm what we already knew: There was no trace of Nonna Eia. We raced back down and went in the house. The flooding had left a layer of mud on the floor, and it was very slippery. The rooms were deserted — I checked the second floor too, even though I knew the tortoise couldn't climb the stairs.

I ran to the shed and found that empty too. The ground was still drenched and muddy. I glanced over at the hole where Nonna had spent such a long time deep in hibernation; there were the miserable remains of my fire. I lifted up what was left of the plastic tent made of ponchos, but I knew already that there'd be nothing underneath.

I went back and joined Mamma. Together we called and called, our voices hoarse with anguish. Night was falling fast. I'd never stayed so late at Nonna's house. Chills went up my spine. Everything around me felt so alien. So solitary, so empty. I groped for Mamma's hand and squeezed it hard.

Chapter Fourteen

There are moments in life when reality splits apart. It's like a curtain torn open, and through the gap you get a glimpse of another kind of reality, something strange and inconceivable.

I had a feeling that Nonna Eia's absence was caused by one of those splits. Too absurd to be true.

"What should we do?" I whispered. It didn't make sense that Nonna would have left of her own free will while we were away. Something must have made her flee. She was hiding from danger. But I couldn't begin to imagine what kind of danger it could be.

"We'll look for her," my mother declared firmly. "She couldn't have gone very far, could she? You know the neighborhood. Which way could she have gone?"

I gazed around, uncertain. The whole area was enclosed by the shipyard's high wall on one side and the lagoon on the other. You couldn't leave except by crossing the footbridge, and in order to reach that, you had to pass in front of the *Casermette*.

"Let's see if we can find any tracks," I said, trying to sound confident as I set out toward the path. Winter had stripped away some of its weeds.

We left the house and the clearing behind and arrived at the shipyard gate.

"Could someone who works here have taken her?" Mamma asked.

"I don't think so. I've never seen anyone go through this gate." I looked around; the flat gray haze of twilight blurred the outlines of the shrubbery. No tracks in sight. We kept on walking.

"Maybe she passed by the *Casermette* while we were in the boat," I said.

Mamma didn't think that was likely. She pointed to the cottages that were visible off in the distance.

"If she did, there'd be some commotion down there. Venetians aren't used to seeing giant tortoises parading past their houses, are they?" She spread out her arms and cried, "She's vanished into thin air!" as if this were a more plausible explanation.

I glanced at her puzzled face. Now she'll decide she was hallucinating, I thought. She'll think the tortoise never existed.

"What's behind there?" She pointed at the thick, tangled undergrowth between the *Casermette* and the shipyard wall.

"I've never been there." It looked like a good hiding place. The problem was, there was no way to get through it. It was all dense and overgrown with brambles, even in winter.

We left the path and headed in that direction. The sky was almost completely dark. Soon night would fall.

"Look!" I seized my mother's arm and clutched it tight.

In the tangled undergrowth was a kind of trail, a place where the shrubs and bushes were flattened out. It led off into the dark.

"She's in there," I said. I was sure of it. I started along that faint trail, and my legs got all scratched up. Mamma followed behind me. The farther I went, the more certain I was that we'd find her. I shoved aside the wild rosebushes and held them apart so the thorny branches wouldn't scrape Mamma's face. We kept going for a while on what we hoped was a path. The trail was getting vaguer all the time, until we found ourselves deep in a thicket of bushes and weeds that closed up behind us, leaving us alone and surrounded.

Darkness was falling very swiftly. I was afraid we'd never be able to find our way out of this tangle. But once we struggled to push aside the clumps of brambles, we located the path again — the grass and weeds were flattened out. A few more steps and we were in a more open space.

I touched a wall on my right. "We're in back of the big shed, I think. Yes, here's a window."

I stopped. Mamma came up close to me to peer inside an opening about five feet above the ground. There was no barbed wire or anything blocking it.

I was right. We were at the back of the huge shed where the

big trucks were kept, that gloomy shed that used to make me think of the Ku Klux Klan each time I passed it going over the footbridge.

Inside, the dark was thick and impenetrable, like a palpable thing giving off cold, hostile vibes.

We stood absolutely still, not making a sound, without the courage to call for Nonna out loud. It was as if instead of our tortoise, something much more ancient, some mysterious, ferocious monster, had taken refuge in the shadows.

But then I heard something encouraging. "She's hiding here. I heard a puffing," I whispered.

"I don't hear anything."

"I did. I'm positive."

We moved away from the window to inch along the wall. A little farther on, we pushed aside the bushes and discovered an opening, all cracked and crumbled. "There's a hole here," I said in a murmur.

Suddenly, a yellow light revealed what was behind the crack in the wall: Mamma had lit a match. The flame flickered for a few seconds, lighting up the scene.

It must have been the back of one of the big trucks, all worn away. I took a step forward and stumbled on a rock. The flame went out. I could feel Mamma's breath behind me. We were inside the shed.

"There's no one here," Mamma whispered.

"Nonna Eia?" I called. I forced myself to speak up loud and clear, to break the spell.

The sound of my voice reverberated around us, eerie and terrifying. We were like two children lost in a haunted castle. The air was icy and damp. It smelled of cat urine. Again we felt a chilly fluttering above our heads. A rustling.

"Bats," Mama whispered, and raised her arms to protect her hair.

Instinctively, I did the same thing. Maybe that was the noise I'd heard before . . . just the sounds of the bats playing tricks on me.

We waited.

"Nonna Eia!"

This time my voice came out choked, much weaker than I had intended. A miserable squeak. Why couldn't I shout out loud? And why wasn't my mom shouting at the top of her lungs?

A puffing sound rose from the dark. It wasn't a bat. Not a bat at all! It was one of those snorts I knew so well. . . .

"Light another match," I pleaded, and when the flame spread its yellowish light, I looked around frantically. The huge tracks cast dancing shadows before my eyes.

Again came the snort, deep and melancholy.

Even Mamma heard it this time. Along with something else. It sounded like the snore of someone fast asleep.

Holding the lit match up high, we moved forward a few steps in the direction of the snore — toward a truck on our left.

Something lay on the ground, a dark heap. We drew close. A man was stretched out on the floor, face down, with his arms clutching a round boulder where he rested his head and shoulders. This was the snorer.

Even though his body was almost completely covering it, I knew at once that the boulder was Nonna.

We stopped a few feet away, paralyzed by fear and relief. The man's face was hidden, but still we recognized immediately that skinny shape and the suede jacket.

Max. Always so tired. Stealing Nonna must have exhausted him. He was clinging to the tortoise in his sleep, as if he was afraid it might escape.

The flame went out before I could tell whether the tortoise was awake or had slipped back into hibernation. I hadn't seen it move.

"That was the last one," Mamma muttered.

"What?"

"The matches are gone. The box is empty!"

I heard the bats flying over our heads again.

There are two of us, I thought wildly. And he's fast asleep. We can do it. We'll jump on top of him, grab hold of him, and . . . and what? Bite him? Kick him? In the dark?

Once more the air above us was stirred by the flurry of

bats' wings. Maybe that was what made me think of a better plan. That, and the fact that Max was fast asleep. I remembered his confession, his terror of nightmares. I went up close to Mamma and put my lips to her ear.

I spoke to her for a long time: There were lots of things she needed to know, lots of lines she had to learn by heart. I repeated them again and again, whispering into the porches of her ear, sending them straight to her brain.

"If you can't remember the words, just make them up! Don't be afraid to improvise! The important thing is the tone. Just yell as loud as you can," I finished up, with an encouraging whisper.

Mamma nodded, too astonished to reply. Maybe she didn't really feel like jumping on top of Max either, so my bizarre plan must have seemed like a good alternative.

In the dark, above the human snoring, I could still hear that oceanic snort. Very light, very faint.

"Now!" I whispered.

I stood up straight and puffed out my chest so my voice would come out full force. Then I yelled, "'I come, Graymalkin!'"

Mamma, alongside me, bellowed in a cavernous voice: "'Fair is foul, and foul is fair. Hover through the fog and filthy air.'"

"'Where hast thou been, sister?'" I trumpeted.

"'Killing swine!'" Mamma's tone was savage, unrecognizable. The echo amplified our screams till they sounded unearthly.

We heard a movement from down where the man was stretched out.

I started screeching nonstop, like a soul possessed. "'Round about the cauldron go; In the poisoned entrails throw! Fillet of a fenny snake, In the cauldron boil and bake.'"

A noise, a long, drawn-out moan.

The bats were freaking out, zooming overhead. I banged my hands on my thighs to make as much of a racket as I could. Smacks and howls.

And at that instant, from down where the man and the tortoise lay, came a fearsome, raucous sound.

I don't think Mamma could make out those thundering words, but I sensed right away what they were. They sounded like, "'By the pricking of my thumbs, Something wicked this way comes.'"

Nonna Eia had awakened! She was joining in! The third witch!

"'Double, double, toil and trouble; Fire burn and cauldron bubble,'" Mamma screeched, adding a satanic burst of laughter worthy of an ogress.

"'Cool it with a baboon's blood, Then the charm is firm and good!'" bellowed the dread voice from down below. Along with the voice came sinister rumbles that seemed to surge up from the depths of hell. I don't know how she produced them, maybe by beating her paws on the ground.

"'Finger of birth-strangled babe,'" Mamma howled. "'Eye of newt, and toe of frog, Wool of bat, and tongue of dog.'" Her cackle was enough to freeze even my blood.

In the dark, the man before us must have sat up. His moan turned into a terrified wailing.

"'For a charm of pow'rful trouble, Like a hell-broth boil and bubble!'"

While I shrieked, part of me was getting a kick out of doing this together with Mamma. She was a fantastic witch, utterly wicked and depraved. My accomplice! With her beside me and Nonna Eia joining in, I felt powerful and invulnerable.

Max must have risen to his feet.

"No, no, no," we heard him yelp incoherently in the dark. "No, no, no! Get away! Get away!"

Mamma and I kept up our menacing, hellish catcalls, and Nonna Eia was busy with her spine-chilling blasts, but I don't think Max was even capable of hearing us anymore. "Go away! Go! Go!" he kept screaming.

Though I couldn't see him, I could imagine him perfectly: his hands over his ears so he wouldn't hear, his body spinning like a top, his head jerking convulsively.

You'll never get rid of us that way, I thought. You better run for it. Go on, run, run!

We heard louder noises, like rocks rolling around, hurrying footsteps, more wails, and still that desperate, constant "Go away! Go away!" like a dog howling, which told us where he was in the dark. He'd moved off. He was retreating.

Like a blind mole flushed out of its burrow, he found his way out. His cries of "No!" and his frenzied shrieks trailed off, till at last they vanished into the night.

We kept up our caterwauling for another minute or so, until none of us had any voice left: The only sounds we could get out were hoarse and shrill. We fell silent, exhausted.

Macbeth's witches had come to our rescue! It didn't matter that we had hopelessly jumbled all the lines: Shakespeare always goes straight for the jugular.

We inched our way forward through the darkness, one step at a time. I leaned down and groped to touch the tortoise, who was moving along with us.

"Nonna!" I cried. I could feel Mamma bending down beside me.

I looked up toward the rustling overhead. High up there in the dark, the bats were careening from one end of the shed to the other. I wasn't afraid of them. They'd been on our side, hadn't they, when we were witches?

"Why did you let him bring you here, Nonna?" I asked, interrupting the loving gestures and murmurs she and Mamma were exchanging. "Why did you go along with Max instead of waiting for us the way we arranged?" I placed a hand on her little head, to feel her presence in the dark.

"HE OFFERED ME A NICE FRESH CARROT AND THEN HE SAID HE COULD TAKE ME TO ALDABRA." The tortoise's voice sounded so garbled, I could hardly grasp what she was saying.

"And you'd go, just like that?" I exclaimed indignantly. "For a nice fresh carrot? Nonna!"

"FOR ALDABRA," she mumbled.

"You would have left us!" I was appalled.

"What's she saying?" Mamma was getting all excited. "Why would she leave us?"

I tried to explain what I thought must have happened. "Max must have followed us from home, Mamma. Either you or me. Then he hid and waited till we went away so he could . . . could trick Nonna. He promised to take her to Aldabra."

"Promised her? You mean he spoke to her? How would he know the tortoise could understand him?"

What Mamma said made me stop and think. She was right; how did it happen? Why would Max speak to her? He couldn't know our tortoise could understand human language . . . unless he'd spied on us from close by, close enough to hear our conversations. . . . But in that case we would have seen him. No, the solution was more simple.

"Max is used to talking to his reptiles. He thinks of them as friends, sort of. He thinks they understand him. He must have done the same thing with the tortoise, tried to persuade her by the sound of his voice," I said.

"And she followed him of her own free will?" My mom sounded bewildered and disappointed. "Where is this Aldabra anyway? I never heard of it. No, no, you'll stay with us, Mamma. We love you with all our hearts. We'll spoil you," she kept urging, a hint of desperation in her voice. "We'll pamper you day and night. Tomorrow is Christmas. Isn't it an amazing coincidence that all three of us are reunited just in time for Christmas?"

In the dark, the tortoise let out a hissing sound. "YEESS-FOOORAWHIIILEYEESSCHRIIISSSTMAAS."

"What did she say?"

"She'll come with us for a little while. For Christmas."

"And then?"

"ALLLDAAABRAAA," the tortoise breathed.

This time I didn't have to act as interpreter. Even my mom understood.

"Aldabra is an atoll in the Indian Ocean," I explained glumly.

"In the Indian Ocean! You must be kidding. How would she get there? It's impossible!"

"We could get some scientist to help us." My words came out dull and lifeless. How homesick Nonna must be for Aldabra, if she'd followed Max simply because he mentioned it! "These tortoises are becoming extinct, an endangered species. They all live there under protection. It's their island. You'll see, the scientists will take her to Aldabra on a ship."

"But it's so far!" In the dark, Mamma's voice sounded even more defeated, more resigned.

"Meanwhile, we've got to get her out of here. We have to get to the boat," I said, to take her mind off Aldabra.

"What about that Max fellow? Isn't he dangerous? What'll we do about him?" Mamma was asking me, as if I were the grown-up and she were the child.

"Nonna, do you think he's still dangerous?" She'd lived with crazy people for a long time; she must know something about them.

Beneath my hand, the little head shook back and forth, meaning no.

"He's far away by now," I said. "Let's not worry about him anymore." I'd learned one thing from Max. I learned that sometimes the people we call crazy are scared, too scared to cope, and so they try to fight off their fear no matter what it takes, regardless of anyone else. That's when they can become dangerous. But our Max would be out of the picture for quite a while. Maybe forever.

We groped our way through the dark until we found the opening in the shed.

Once outside, we were taken by surprise to see a soft glimmer. A round, solid moon, brilliant white, shone in the sky.

The tortoise went ahead at her slow, stately pace, clearing us a path through the curtain of bushes and brambles. We followed behind and got past the thicket without too much trouble, till finally a beam of light from a streetlamp appeared before us. Before long, we could feel the smooth pavement underfoot, and soon we reached the moored boat.

After Nonna Eia managed to climb aboard, we tossed Mamma's heavy coat over her to hide her.

Suddenly, the silence of the night was broken by a whirring sound: Mamma had started the engine.

We glided through the dark waters of the lagoon, smooth as oil. In the moonlight, the wake we left behind gleamed like black gold.

"Nonna, are you okay down there? You're not too cold?"

"We'll be home soon," said Mamma. "You'll be nice and warm."

In response, from under the coat came a puff of air as gentle as a breeze. It was right there beside us, in the boat that was taking us home. And yet it seemed to come from far-off oceans, from lost continents, from distant stars. The fragrance of jasmine and spices mingled with the smell of seaweed and debris deep down in the water flowing beneath us. It was a sweet, suffocating smell. I tried to breathe very lightly so as not to smell it, but after a few moments I was doing just the opposite. To tell the truth, I was gulping it down in deep breaths, my mind blank, not a thought in my head.

Epilogue

The ship sails through the green expanse of choppy water known as the Indian Ocean. It's been days and days since we've sighted any other vessel.

I've been throwing up for the whole trip. Mamma's been throwing up. Nonna Eia, on the other hand, has shown no sign of seasickness. She's found a nook between the cables on the deck and lies there dozing day and night. Allan hasn't been seasick either; he doesn't mind the waves one bit.

Allan is the young American scientist who answered our letter. After lots of phone calls he came to see us in Venice at the end of January and immediately made friends with Nonna Eia. Of course, he doesn't know she's my grandmother. He ruled out the theory that she escaped from a zoo; he's convinced that she got to the lagoon in Venice by swimming straight from her atoll, traveling with the currents. Why Venice? Why, because it has a lagoon, just like Aldabra! A big beautiful lagoon. If a *Geochelone gigantea* can swim from Madagascar to Aldabra (this has been proven, since that's where they came from originally), then why not from Aldabra to Venice? As soon as he returns to the United States, he's going to write an important scientific article on the subject.

Allan is really nice. To thank us for consulting him, he got permission for us to join him on the long voyage, so we could accompany the tortoise to its new home.

"It's an excellent specimen of the male," he told us the first time he saw it. We were in our apartment, and Nonna Eia was roaming around the house, a bit chilly and impatient to set off. She'd grown even bigger those last few weeks by bingeing on panettone.

"No, you're mistaken," I said. "It's a female."

"No, no, it's a male. There are three ways you can tell. Look: The plastron underneath is curved, while the female's is flat; the tail is longer in the males, and the talons are shorter because they don't have to scoop holes in the sand to bury their eggs, like the female."

I peered sideways over at my mother, who caught my glance and merely rolled her eyes toward the ceiling in silence. As if to say: Nonna Eia never ceases to surprise us. Did she really have to turn into a male? Wasn't it enough to turn into a tortoise?

A little later that day, I asked Nonna straight out if it was true that she'd become a male.

"AS LONG AS I WAS AT IT, WHY NOT?" she replied, bringing her paw to the top of her head. "YOU KNOW

HOW MUCH I ALWAYS LIKED PLAYING THE MALE ROLES — OTHELLO, HENRY IV, MACBETH, HAMLET . . ."

So now we're on board this ship bouncing through the waves.

Allan just came to tell us — we're almost at Aldabra. We can't see it yet because it's so flat, but it's only a few miles away. We just have to wait for high tide so we can enter its waters and approach the shore.

With my stomach churning, I come out on deck and lean on the railing. From her corner between the cables, Nonna Eia greets me with a puff of air.

I wish this trip would never end, even though it makes me so sick. But we're almost there. I glance over at Nonna. She raises herself upright on her paws, her neck outstretched, on the alert.

Nonna, Nonna, who'll listen to you perform Shakespeare from now on? I'm worried that if she can't act out some good play to a rapt audience now and then, she'll end up forgetting she was ever human. She'll end up forgetting us. I curl my fingers over the *murrina* of the ring I wear around my neck all the time. I'll never forget you, Nonna. But what about you?

"Look up there," my mother calls out, pointing a finger in the air.

With my head slightly spinning from seasickness and melancholy, I look up.

There's the sky, way up above. So vast and blue — it seems to swallow us up. And in the midst of it, right overhead, in all that dizzying blueness, a green shape stands out, an emerald heart. It's a strange sight, that green heart surrounded by so much blue.

I can't take my eyes off it.

"That's Aldabra," says Allan, right next to me. "It's the reflection of the lagoon on the moist layers of the atmosphere. We're lucky — it's an extremely rare phenomenon. An explorer described it in 1742, but there's no record of anyone seeing it since then."

I turn toward the tortoise. Her neck is stretched up too, as she gazes at the sky. Slowly she raises one paw and brings it to her little reptile head. Her jaws part and she waits, open-mouthed, for that big bite of land mirrored in the sky.

This book was art directed
and designed by Elizabeth B. Parisi.
The display text was set in Rapture Heavenly
and Nicholas Cochin.
The body text was set in Centaur.
This book was printed and bound by Berryville
Graphics, Virginia.